The
Eden Book Society
100 Years of Unseen Horror

PLUNGE HILL

A CASE STUDY

J.M. McVulpin

First published in 1972
by The Eden Book Society

The Eden Book Society

First published in Great Britain in 2020 by The Eden
Book Society, an imprint of Cinder House Publishing Limited.

ISBN 978-1-911585-48-0

Printed and bound in Great Britain by Clays Ltd,
Elcograf S.p.A.

www.edenbooksociety.com

www.deadinkbooks.com

About the Society

Established in 1919, The Eden Book Society was a private publisher of horror for nearly 100 years. Presided over by the Eden family, the press passed through the generations publishing short horror novellas to a private list of subscribers. Eden books were always published under pseudonyms and, until now, have never been available to the public.

Dead Ink Books is pleased to announce that it has secured the rights to the entire Eden Book Society backlist and archives. For the first time, these books, nearly a century of unseen British horror, will be available to the public. The original authors are lost to time, but their work remains and we will be faithfully reproducing the publications by reprinting them one year at a time.

We hope that you will join us as we explore the evolving fears of British society as it moved through the 20th century and eventually entered the 21st. We begin our reproduction with 1972, a year of exciting and original horror for the Society.

J.M. McVulpin

J.M. McVulpin was born in 1911. He was educated at Stonyhurst College, Lancashire, and read Medicine at University College, London before going on to establish a career in psychiatry in the north of England. He was a consultant psychiatrist in hospitals across Lancashire and Cumbria, including Clitheroe, Pendle, Windhaven and Plunge Hill. His monographs include *Diagnosis Hysteria*, *Birth Trauma Conditioning* and *The Insulin Shock Therapy Handbook*. After the initial publication of his controversial final work, *Plunge Hill: A Case Study* by The Eden Book Society in 1972, he retired from practice and relocated to Argentina. As a result of an intervention by the then Health Secretary Sir Keith Joseph, Plunge Hill Hospital closed its doors late in that same year. McVulpin is believed to have drowned off the coast of Bertioga, Brazil in 1979.

'In an age of investigation like our own, when we are returning to science as the base of wonders – almost of miracles – we should be slow to refuse to accept facts, however impossible they may seem to be.'

Bram Stoker, *The Lair of the White Worm*

Editor's Preface

The lesson, such as it is, to be gleaned from what you are about to read is a stark one: beware fiction.

Bridget Shipley's pathology was hidden, a bud that bloomed in darkness. While she diligently performed her administrative duties at Plunge Hill Hospital, she sank deeper and deeper into the quagmire of her own particular disorder – a disorder unnoticed by those around her, and tragically untreated by those who were best placed to help. Late last year, she took her own life. The gruesome and violent circumstances of her death have been widely reported and the prurient reader may consult the articles published in the gutter press for more detail at their own risk. I will not reproduce them here.

In the immediate aftermath of Bridget's suicide, I heard rumours concerning a number of papers she'd left behind: letters, a diary, and handfuls of postcards. I confess that my initial sympathy swiftly gave way to professional intrigue: I imagined that these documents, if they existed, would provide a rare, direct insight into the flowering of a mania few professionals find themselves in a position to study. I immediately determined to locate them and construct a kind of case study from them. Bridget's landlady, and later on, her parents, both supplied me with the material I asked for. You hold in your hands now the case study that resulted from my work.

It feels appropriate, while I detain you with these prefatory remarks, to stress that I did not know Bridget Shipley personally. This may surprise the reader, but any functioning hospital is like a heart, its chambers and ventricles sealed and separated from one another yet working in a co-ordinated and greater harmony. I cannot be expected to know precisely what takes place in the surgical theatres, the kitchens and the laundry rooms. I have never inspected the maternity wards and the dark art of gynaecology remains a mystery to me. My own 'ventricle', so to speak, affords a lofty view down the hill towards Plunge Hill itself, the small, charming village by which our hospital is – or was, I suppose I should say – fortunate enough to be located, and, as such, I have, during my time here, been provided with nothing in the way of direct insight into the workings of the typing pool, where Bridget spent her final weeks. Although she was not my patient, the Hippocratic Oath lead me to conceive of the notion of letting her papers lie unedited, hidden and unknown – as her suffering was during her life – as something tantamount to a kind of professional neglect on my part.

There is a further motivation for the present case study. News of Bridget's tragic end – her body found in most vivid and unfortunate circumstances in the well-tended grounds of the hospital – could not escape my attention. I also became aware – in common with you, dear reader – of the fabrications and speculations about her final weeks. I feared – as did Dr Kapoor, my colleague and friend – that these stories not only slandered Bridget's name, causing unnecessary pain to her suffering parents, but risked doing damage to the greater mission of Plunge Hill Hospital itself. I trust the reader will encounter in the present volume a curative to such salacious nonsense. Although, of course, in many ways it is now too late.

To return to my opening words of warning – beware fiction – it behoves me to expand. Many years of clinical experience have taught me this: manic and deluded patients, the ones who project their squalid obsessions onto the everyday, carve paranoid fantasises from unremarkable interactions and weave extravagant conspiracy theories from happenstance, who accuse those around them of the very lunacy from which they themselves suffer – well, frequently they can seem very credible. It is crucial to remember that. Freud reminds us, 'from error to error, one discovers the entire truth,' and my aim here is to present the web of Bridget's errors so that we may advance together upon a more rarefied strain of truth: the intricate mechanics of a mangled mind.

Thus the case study in question is presented to you in the guise of a collage of reticulated documents which, assessed collectively, reveal a young woman traumatised by unresolved guilt and grief. They may assist us in developing therapeutic treatments and preventative measures in the future, perhaps. The ground-breaking form of this paper – presenting the patient almost entirely in her own words – has perhaps been the reason several less intellectually courageous editors have been unwilling to publish it. To the dusty, timid minds at *Psychological Methods*, *The Clinical Psychology Review*, *Focus on Psychiatry* and *The Couch* – many of whom I have been assured are esteemed Eden Book Society subscribers of long standing – I say this: read on for a taste of a brave new direction of our profession. Consider this slim volume my Grand Rounds – with young Bridget herself as present for questions as she is able to be.

Bridget Shipley – 'Brix' to her friends – was led tragically astray by her delusions of Plunge Hill, and yet this village is a place of peace and delight. I shall be sad to leave. Indeed, this tragedy has been a wide-ranging one, young Bridget's death having ripple-like effects on almost everyone who made their home here, myself included.

The air is fresh and healthful around here, even in spite of the intrusive clouds of dust, propelled through the building's interior by the wholesale removal of equipment and furniture which is currently taking place. Tradesmen are noisily packing up and taking away everything – I can hear them now in the corridor beyond my office door, voices and movement, a metal trolley clanging as boxes are piled onto it – yet when I open my window and breathe in deeply I cannot help but feel at ease, a sense that I am safe, here in my allotted upper ventricle of the hospital, no matter what may come. The end of Plunge Hill may be at hand, but the gardens are in fine fettle, and the rhododendrons are coming into bloom after their lengthy winter dormancy. My nanny always said their blossoms smelled like blood and honey. The frenzy and urgency of their fertility is invigorating.

J.M. McVulpin
Consultant Psychiatrist
Plunge Hill Hospital, Spring 1972

A postcard donated by Mr and Mrs Shipley,[1] *showing the front aspect of Plunge Hill Hospital: at either side of the frame is one of a pair of tall pillars between which opens up the long, straight driveway which cuts through the gardens up to the hospital building, a late Georgian infirmary, imposing yet charming in its simplicity, a large block consisting of neat rows of mullioned windows, the only ornamentation an additional pair of pillars at either side of the front entrance atop which sits a large triangular lintel bearing the legend (illegible in this image) SUPERVIVIT APTISSIMUS. The gardens themselves are a charming combination of prettiness and unfussiness, the trimmed lawns and the neat and lofty shrubbery are the picture of restraint alongside flowerbeds rioting with lurid alliums, oriental poppies and silverswords. The day appears to be bright, the*

1   Future items will be marked 'Shipley collection' for those materials sent to London by Bridget. Other items, retrieved from her residence in Plunge Village and donated by Miss Liversall, will be marked 'Liversall collection'.

weather brisk but not too cold, perhaps late autumn. In short, the quintessence of serious, elegant salubriousness. Condition: fair to good. Postcard is not addressed – date is given as 2nd October 1971. No stamp or postmark. Left and right halves have been used for the message addressed to Maurice Shipley from his older sister, Bridget. Bridget sent the postcard to Maurice inside an envelope (one presumes for privacy) which has since been discarded or lost.

Maurice,

Am resplendent at my new desk, mechanical pencil sharpener standing ready for duty on my left, a tray of carbon paper to my right. All set. Can you believe they were selling these postcards in the hospital gift shop? Suggested it was some kind of joke, given the actual state of the place – and the shop assistant (v. dour) tutted at me. Tell Mum and Dad I've landed. Got my coins in the payphone but lost my nerve before dialling. Don't worry. I will be fine. Will write to you so often you will be sick to death of me, I promise.

Brix.

Plunge Hill: A Case Study

❦ ❦ ❦

Article is a typed letter tucked inside a rather gauche greetings card. Front colour panel shows an old fashioned teddy bear holding a red balloon. Inside, the legend reads 'Congratulations' and has been crossed through. Condition: poor. Envelope missing. Undated. Shipley Collection.

Maurice – won't you write? Send it to the hospital and the porters will bring it and put it in my in-tray and it will get me through another day of filing. I didn't sleep well last night. The old dreams again. But it will settle down – it's just being in a new place.

You have to imagine me drowning in reams of patient records, all full of crabby doctors' writing, in the middle of a huge and bustling typing pool. There's only one desk, next to mine, which is vacant. And Maurice, it is *gloomy*. I don't even have a window to look out of. There's just one floor beneath us (the lower basement) with some old offices and archives and (shudder!) the mortuary – but even the 'upper basement' is underground too, because of the hill. Today it feels like not only the whole hospital – all the wings and wards and beds and sick people – is weighing down on top of me, but the hill itself is leaning against the back of the building and pushing – *pushing* – and that, and not my sleepless night, is the real reason I've got a bit of a headache.[2]

Let me tell you about where I live. There was no phone number on the letter from the hospital, just the address of the place I was to present myself, should I accept the position. I made my way there straight from the train station. It was dark by the time I knocked on the door and an old woman answered. She was a bony little thing with a severe overbite and eyes that were both screwed up tight, and flitted around the entire time – as if she was both furious about some infraction, and busily looking out for the next offense.

'So you're the one who they've given her room to.' She looked me up and down, evidently displeased by the sight before her. 'Come in then, come in!' She primped her hair, already sounding impatient and I silently followed her in, walking slowly behind her as she winced and shuffled

---

2   Bridget's body was examined in the usual way after her death by my former colleague, Dr Parag Kapoor. His reports (not reproduced here for the sake of brevity) confirm that the patient showed no signs of tumor, epilepsy, congenital deformation nor infection: one wonders if these headaches were psychosomatic, and perhaps the first symptom of her incipient illness.

her way down the hallway. The place looks like it's not been done up in a hundred years: wall lamps, threadbare carpet, dark and heavy curtains streaked with dust. Loads of houseplants hanging in the windows: all of them dead or dying.

'You may address me as Miss Liversall,' she said. 'This way.' She started up the stairs, dragging herself upwards, hand over hand on the bannister. 'No pets, no overnight guests. The front door is bolted at 9:00pm. 9:30pm on Fridays. I can leave leftovers which you're welcome to eat, but only in the kitchen and only provided you leave it as spotless as you find it.'

We got upstairs, onto a narrow landing lined with closed doors. 'I'll boil an extra egg in the morning if asked the night before, but only if asked,' she said, a hand on her hip as if she was in pain. She pointed at the doors one by one, wheezing and out of breath. 'Bathroom. Airing cupboard. My bedroom – you're not to go in there, understand? Your room.'

In we went. Single bed. Brown curtains at the window and a wicker shade. It was spotless, Maurice – but spotless in the way a prison cell or hospital is. I shivered.

'There's none of this central heating in this house,' she said, 'so you'll have to make sure you keep wrapped up same as I do.' She looked at me again, as if inspecting my blouse and skirt, then nodded. 'You'll be starting at the hospital in the morning,' she said.

'That's right,' I said. 'A typist.'

'And you are all prepared?'

I must have looked a bit bedraggled after the train journey and the trudge from the station through the little village. It's right what they say about the North you know – the wind, the rain – the air was so heavy with mist it felt impossible to breathe – as if I was drowning on dry land.

'If there's an iron I could borrow? Perhaps? In the morning?' I said. This seemed to satisfy her, as she nodded, then left.

So that's home sweet home for the time being. I wouldn't exactly call it a warm welcome. But I will get used to it. I'll learn to charm her if it kills me!

Anyway, how are you doing, little man? I won't assume you got my postcard. I'm guessing Mum and Dad are still angry. But you mustn't worry about anything except getting better: eat up extra helpings of pudding and sleep as long as you can and keep yourself warm and you'll be right as rain. I know it. I'm almost a medic already: type up enough of this stuff and it seeps into your brain. I could diagnose an arthritic seaside donkey, given five minutes and a look at his notes!!!!

The work here isn't quite what I thought it would be. Most of the time I'm just typing up the minutes of meetings I never went to, or moving patient records from one end of the hospital to the other. Do you know what they give me to cart the files about on? You won't guess. Just imagine me, if you can, at the helm of an old hospital bed, one wonky wheel, loaded up with files, slipping around as I turn the corners. I expected they'd have some special work for me to do. They were the ones who wrote to me and asked me to come.[3] But there's nothing. It is boring and I bet it's even more boring to read about so I'll stop there.

I have been able to get out a little bit. Into the grounds. There are some gardens where the patients who need fresh air can get wheeled about by their nurses. You can't get around the back of the hospital because the building kind

---

3   Note here the beginnings of Bridget's delusion. She claims that she has been invited, perhaps hand-chosen, for this lowly role. This is a quite typical example of grandiose delusions – compare the case of Patient T, who believed that the Queen was writing to him to invite him to an audience at Buckingham Palace, but that his father was intercepting the letters. *Annals of Psychiatry* (McVulpin and Kapoor, 1965).

of melts into the hill so we all pace back and forth along the front. You feel like you're on display, or being watched from the windows the entire time. And the gardens are a right state: nothing like the way they are in the postcard I sent.

It's the wrong time of year, I suppose. Most of the grass is dead: the lawns just waterlogged and mossy, the flowerbeds bare and the shrubbery drooping. It is so wet here I am not surprised they have trouble getting things to grow. Chapcott – she's my boss – told me they're going to make some improvements to the grounds and we'll all be seeing the hospital's 'front aspect return to its former glory very soon,' but I'll believe that when I see it.

Bugger. 'Scuse my French. The other typists are back from lunch now. Gaggle of them. Can't be bothered naming them all for you, so imagine a flock of drab birds – all tweed coats and pink lipstick. Predictably, they're all as thick as thieves and if there's a dusty, horrible, boring job to do it will be the new girl, the Southerner, odd bird out, who has to do it. This afternoon I'm sorting filing cabinets. Thought it was a joke at first. A personal invitation to come here and they have me sorting filing cabinets behind the empty desk next to mine. Still, it's not all bad. I found a box of Black Magic in the bottom drawer of my own desk this morning.

I'm pretending it's a present from the girl who was here before me – a little gift to welcome me to the team. Because nobody else bloody cares. When she – the girl I replaced – wrote up notes she initialled the bottom corner of each page: A.N – and so I've been calling her An and chattering away to her as I push my bed full of files around the corridors. I think I've lost the plot through sheer boredom.[4]

Listen, Maurice. If Dad asks after me, make up something glamorous. Tell him I've been promoted to personal assistant for the best consultant in here already, and that I spend all my time arranging fancy dinners and shielding him from patients who have fallen hopelessly in love with him.

Brix.

❦   ❦   ❦

Greetings card. Front colour panel depicts a cot. In blue writing: The Stork Has Visited! Inside: 'Congratulations on your new Delivery', crossed through. Condition: poor. Significant water damage. Shipley collection.

---

4   Indeed.

J.M. McVulpin

Excuse the card, Maurice. Needs must, and I like puzzling the old dragon that sells them to me. About my friend An. She had long blonde hair just like me: I can tell from the hairbrush she left in the top drawer of my desk. I've eaten all her chocolates and used her hand cream and changed the ribbon on her typewriter and today – guess what – I found her diary! Sorting out those bloody filing cabinets. It was tucked in under a pile of old used-up carbon paper, wrapped in a pink and white patterned headscarf. Hidden – not mislaid, definitely. It's a big thick leather-bound book – not the kind of thing you'd forget about or leave behind accidentally. I read the first page or two kneeling on the floor in front of the open drawer, then tucked it away in my bag before anyone caught me with it. It is stealing – though not from the hospital – the book doesn't belong to Plunge Hill, does it? I am going to read a page or two each night before I try to nod off. Maybe it will keep the bad dreams away. It feels like making a new friend.

B x x x

❧   ❧   ❧

Plunge Hill: A Case Study

Anouk's diary, March 15th 1971. Extracted from a leather-bound book,[5] unruled. Liversall collection.

At Dr Kapoor's suggestion, every day I am going to spend my lunch break writing in you, small notebook, for to improve my written English. No, every day I am going to write in this notebook to improve my English. No for. It is not needed. You see, already I am learning!

I am Anouk. Hello. How do you do? Pleased to meet you. I hope you are well. Good morning. This is the BBC.

I live in 33 Ives Road, Plunge Hill, England. My full name is Anouk Nykvist, although the other girls who work here say I should change it to Anna Nichols to 'fit in'. I tell them that Dr Kapoor hasn't changed his name. He is still Parag Kapoor, not Patrick Cooper. They look at me as though I have said something shocking. This, they tell me, is because he is a doctor and doctors do not have to worry about fitting in.

I am not a doctor. I am not even a nurse. I am a typist. The girls are all typists. I go through Dr Kapoor's notes and type them up so real nurses and other doctors can read them. Not a very exciting job or one which sounds

---

5   Leather bound notebooks of this type are sold in the village post office.

very important, but this is why my English needs to be good. I have to know the language so I can type it. 'An incorrect word here or there could cost a life, Anouk,' says Mrs Chapcott.

Mrs Chapcott had said, 'I'm Head Girl,' when first I met her. She said it with a laugh and I laughed also but I did not understand her joke. And her other words, about minor errors costing lives, leave me unsettled. For one thing, the doctors have terrible handwriting in England, all of them, worse than mine. I asked Mrs Chapcott why this was and she told me it was deliberate, that the doctors are all writing like that so that their handwriting cannot be copied. Also, I understand very little of what I write. Here, for example, is a brief example copied from this morning's typing.

Await further results but so far indications suggest post-mortem human blood no use. Consider introducing sus scrofa domesticus to H: comparable μm and mil/ll to human RBC. But would H be receptive? Environmental factors must be taken into consideration when preparing. Introduction must be v. gradual. Suggest 0.25 fluid ounces per pt. blood initially. To dilute: one hour min. Easter v. soon.

Do you see? How am I to know whether this is correct or not? I do not understand Dr Kapoor's work. I know him to be doing important research into blood, but the *apheresis*, the *exsanguination*, the *haematophage*, I do not understand these terms.

It is very shocking to me that this Dr Kapoor can come into the office to begin work dressed very smartly in a suit with a tie and an ironed shirt then, later in the day, he will emerge out of his surgery wearing overalls, gloves and a cotton mask over his face, all of them covered with blood, some of it looking very red but some of it looking very brown, as though it were there a long time ago and has been left. Dressed like this he will stride out and drop a large collection of notes onto my desk. Sometimes there will be a bloody thumbprint on the outer sheet from where he has been holding it. I find this frightening – it is as though it sets something in the corner of my mind humming – but none of the other girls seem to think it frightening. They chatter among themselves about the upcoming Easter Parade, clearly in awe of this man but otherwise oblivious to his most ghoulish appearance.

So, to fit in, I pretend I also do not find it frightening and simply get on with typing up Dr Kapoor's incomprehensible notes. The sound of this place, all of us click clacking away down here, can be so very noisy. And there are no windows onto the outside world here, only the heat from the furnaces below us.

I do not know if the other girls like me. I am writing this in the canteen on my own. The other typists all sit together, eating and talking and laughing and occasionally they look over at me, but there is not space enough for another chair at their table. But I am used to this. I have grown comfortable being on the outside.

Dr Kapoor is a very nice man. I have come to understand that this is one of the greatest compliments one can receive here in England: *a nice man*. And he is a nice man. And yet, as this diary is for myself alone, I feel I can write perhaps down thoughts I would be unlikely to share. As such, let me state that there is something about Dr Kapoor which I find I do not like. It is hard for me to be precise as this entire place – Plunge Hill, England, its North – is so strange. I cannot find the correct words for him. It is not just the blood on his clothes, although that does underline this strangeness of his. The closest I can think of in Swedish is he is *blåsväder*: bad weather, bad news – something perhaps dark and stormy, but too much on the distant horizon to be sure, too far away.

Ah, but I see my hour is up! The other girls are getting up, making their way back to our basement. I will permit myself a further brief burst of Swedish. How I miss it.

Plunge Hill: A Case Study

Tiden går fort när man har roligt. Or, as I have learnt the English have it: how the time flies when you are having fun.

𝆏 𝆏 𝆏

Postcard, showing a rolling field of daffodils in bloom. Undated. Shipley collection.

The countryside round here will look like this when the spring comes, Maurice – or so they tell me. There's framed pictures of last year's Easter Parade up in the lobby of the hospital: all flower bonnets and sombre faces. But spring is a very long way away and for now there's just mud and mist and dark afternoons. I found the little chapel in the hospital today: a tiny room with folding wooden chairs and a crucifix hung up on an unpainted wall. I sat down and unwrapped my sandwiches. An old man came, pushing a cleaning trolley.

'Sorry Miss, didn't mean to disturb you at your reflections,' he said.

'Oh no,' I replied, glad of the company, 'I wasn't praying. Just…' I gestured towards the remains of my lunch, '…just having a break.'

'Thinking about your little brother?' he said as if he'd caught me doing something unprofessional – something despicable and wrong. He sniffed. 'I'll leave you to it,' he said, and went.

I was thinking about the daffodils, actually. But a hospital is like a big family, Mrs Chapcott says, and nothing here is secret. I suppose it's not so strange that they've taken the time to check my references and find out a little bit about me. But it feels strange.

Later on I made a mistake. I'd idly left a couple of pieces of paper on the empty desk next to mine. I noticed a couple of the other girls turning their heads to look, their typing stopping.

'What?' I asked. 'What is it?'

By that time, Mrs Chapcott had marched across to me and removed the offending sheets, placing them back on my desk.

'Please do see that you keep your work to your own desk.'

'Sorry,' I said. 'I didn't think anyone was sat there. Is one of the girls off sick?'

'It's really rather tragic, actually,' she said. 'One of our girls passed away earlier this year. Gloria, she was called. There was an accident. But in many ways she's with us still, giving us health and strength. It's heartbreaking to lose one of our own. We like to keep her desk clear, out of respect.'

And with that she sallied away.

B.

❧ ❧ ❧

Anouk's diary, entry dated as previously, later that same day.

So here I am, back home in my room at Ives Road, filling space, killing time. Shall I write my life story? My family life is nothing much to speak of. My mother passed away (how I love these sad, evasive phrases the English use to say what they mean) many years ago. I have very few memories of her. My father is alive, but we do not speak. I suppose he must have struggled on his own. He drank. There was no grand argument. We were never close and simply parted as I grew older. I moved out when I could, to Uppsala, a city close to my home, and met Clive, a boy from Britain. A man, I should say. He had a moustache of curly black hair and always wore pointy boots of shiny leather. He drove a lorry and was heading back home, to the north of England. 'Newcastle' he said, and the name sounded wonderful to me, so evocative: a grand, ancient, solid English castle, but somehow swinging and new. It occurred to me that I could start again; I too could be English – old and wise yet born anew. And so Clive with the curly moustache took me in his lorry to Newcastle where I lived with him for a time.

But I struggled to understand what people said, and they to understand me. I worked here and there, in a newspaper shop, in a pornographic cinema, as a cleaner. But nothing lasted very long. There was always some reason to let me go, some oversight I had unwittingly committed, and some local who had been promised my job. Curiously, it was while I was not working that I received a letter. I had found myself in a bad situation – very bad – and I had nowhere to live but was instead sleeping on the sofa of a friend (Clive and I had not lasted). The letter was from the Board of Health and informed me there was a vacancy for a typist at a hospital in a village called Plunge Hill for which I had been selected. This I found curious. I had not applied for the job, nor even been in touch with the hospital. I had not even heard of Plunge Hill. It is not the way of things in Sweden, but I suppose it must be here in

England, and who is Anouk to turn down a job? And so I said goodbye to Newcastle and hello to Plunge Hill. And I came from the North East to the North West, to a job of endlessly typing about *transfusions*, *plasma* and *H*.

I did not expect I'd spend so much time alone here, so much of it in the company of my own thoughts. I do not like it. Miss Liversall, my landlady, is moving around downstairs. She sings while she takes care of her plants: a lullaby – the words sound as though they are about blood in a well... strange, but then the English are strange. Soon she will turn the lights out. I suppose it is late. I should sleep.

❧   ❧   ❧

Letter, handwritten. Undated. Liversall Collection.

Dear Maurice,

I went out into the village last night. I say village: there's not much there. The flowerbeds are bare, the hanging baskets empty and the tree on the green has already lost its leaves. Even the pub – The Red Pony, it's called – was shut; the doors bolted and the windows dark.

I was about to turn back when I noticed lights on in the windows of the post office. There's a noticeboard in the window. Lost cats, cleaning and ironing offered, second hand cots for sale, etc. I was looking at it, the rain trickling down the back of my neck, when someone standing inside opened the door and gave me quite a fright.

'You're Miss Liversall's new one, aren't you?' a voice said, and, short of company and with nobody else to talk to, I only nodded and went in.

These people are so bloody weird. Four of them, each about a thousand years old – kind of preserved looking – with clouds of white hair and wrinkled faces, and if it hadn't have been for their clothes I don't think I'd have been able to tell the men apart from the women. All sitting hunched over at stools at the post office counter playing hands of Canasta and drinking bottles of beer.

'Oh, I…' I sounded like a complete loony, no doubt. Felt like I was interrupting something. But they were just chatting – something to do with the weather, the way the clouds were gathering up around the hills and spilling down low into the valley – and nobody looked surprised to see me.

'I've cashed up for tonight,' one of them said. She had a purple and orange turban around her white hair, and was leaning against the counter, looking over the card game. 'But if there's something in particular…'

'She won't want anything,' another one said. A man, this time. He smiled at me: his face as crumpled as a raisin. Then I recognised him: the man who'd disturbed me at my lunch in the chapel that day – obviously in a better mood today.

'No. I was just getting some fresh air and…'

They chuckled, understanding, I think, how desperately bored and lonely and in need of company I was. And they introduced themselves. Mrs Appleyard – the lady in the turban – runs the post office and lives above it. Her friend, Mrs Maywell, works in the hospital canteen. Grumpy Mr Blackheath had been a porter at the hospital pretty much since it opened and was planning to retire as soon as the power cuts were over because of his slipped disc or rotator cuff or something. 'Wear and tear, my love,' he croaked. 'Comes to us all one way or another.' Mr Blackheath the second (the first Mr Blackheath's younger brother) only nodded and didn't speak at all, but did odd shifts behind the bar at The Red Pony, and all of them together, the (drum roll, please!) Post Office Canasta Club.

Jesus Christ, Maurice. Don't tell Mum and Dad any of this. Tell them I get the train in to Manchester at the weekend. No, tell them my fancy consultant friend drives me there in his shiny black car, and we go shopping and eat at The French Room.[6] Oh God, tell them what you like – but don't tell them about the Canasta Club. I'm being a horrible, nasty, ungrateful little snob, I know. I know I am. I stayed and played cards with them anyway. Isn't that terrible of me? It was either that or Liversall and her evening radio soap operas.

'Tell us about yourself, Bridget Shipley,' Mrs Appleyard said. She was old – very old – but her eyes were bright and I got the sense not a lot happened in that village that she didn't know about. 'You're behaving yourself, aren't you? You mustn't trouble poor Miss Liversall. Her hip's not what it was.'

---

6   The literature on confabulations of these types tells us the symptom performs two functions for the psyche of the patient – first, a defense against depression and low self-esteem, and second, an after-the-fact explanation for exaggerated and keenly experienced emotions. We can't blame Bridget here, I don't think, for seeking comfort in her solitude – especially knowing what horror and grief lay only too recently behind her. Compare the case of Patient O (McVulpin et al, 1963) a bored and isolated housewife who convinced herself, and her husband, that she was being pursued romantically by the local greengrocer. Patient O's husband now resides at Broadmoor, having been so compelled by his wife's confabulations that he broke into the poor greengrocer's house and slit his throat in front of his wife and baby daughter. Patient O lives quietly. A most intriguing case.

There was a general nodding and shaking of heads and a kind of wheezing of laughter at this comment. I smiled too. When in Rome, etcetera.

'I'm no trouble at all. I go to the hospital, I come back, I eat, I sleep.'

They all nodded, impossibly pleased by this.

'And where were you before? London?'

'That's right.'

'We knew it was London. Your voice. You talk funny.'

'Do I?'

'Mrs Chapcott likes to get a bit of foreign blood into the hospital, doesn't she?' Blackheath-with-the-rotator-cuff said. Mrs Maywell scowled at him but I didn't mind. I suppose I *am* foreign to them.

'Your mum and dad going to come up and see you? See where you work?' she asked.

'I shouldn't think so.'

'And they aren't expecting you back home for a visit? It'll be Christmas before you know it! You not made arrangements to go home?'

'We're not close. Not really.'

I was finding it difficult to do anything other than stare into my teacup at this point, but they didn't seem to notice.

'Well never mind. We do Christmas early here in the village,' Mrs Maywell said.

'Ada…'

'There's no harm in giving her something to look forward to, is there?' Blackheath-the-younger turned to me. It was the first time I'd heard him speak. 'Second week in December – that's when we put our lights up.'

A strange silence fell over them.

'Do you have a party?' I finally asked, trying to hold my end of the conversation up.

Blackheath-the-younger nodded. 'Aye, we do. It's that dark round here, we can't wait until the 25th. We'd be half dead by then if we put it off,' he laughed mirthlessly. 'So we have the Winter Lights. It's only a bit of a knees-up at the Red Pony, then a torchlight walk through the village out to the—'

'It's traditional,' Mrs Maywell said, as if I was disputing the point.

'Will I come to the party? I don't really know anyone yet,' I said.

'You mustn't worry,' Mrs Maywell said, waving a bejewelled hand in my direction. She was fat and pale, and despite her pink jumper and patterned skirt, looked a little bedraggled: almost depressed. 'You'll be more than welcome.'

'I'll look forward to it. I've not really made many friends here yet. The other typists…'

Mrs Appleyard smiled. 'Yes, they do keep themselves to themselves, don't they? But they should be nice to you. Tell Mrs Chapcott if you have any trouble with them. She'll want to know.'

'Fat lot of good that'll do,' Mrs Maywell said, darkly. 'If she'd looked after the other one a bit better, then she wouldn't have—'

Mrs Appleyard put a hand on Mrs Maywell's arm – squeezed it, in fact, and hard, because whatever she was about to say died on her lips. The other one. They meant Anouk, I suppose, who like me was lonely, and wrote about it in her diary.

'You mustn't listen to Ada,' Mrs Appleyard said.

'She's tapped,' one of the Misters Blackheath said. 'She's tapped in the head. Brain's gone rancid.'

Mrs Maywell looked downcast, then took a long drink from her beer and wouldn't look at me. I realised, counting up the empty bottles on the counter, that the lot of them were very, very drunk. The Blackheath men dealt a fresh hand and the awkwardness passed, until I opened my mouth and plunged us all right back into it.

'Did any of you know the girl who rented the room

before I did? She was from Sweden, wasn't she?' I asked. 'That's *real* foreign blood!'

The Blackheath men glowered. Mrs Appleyard busied herself straightening the cosy on the teapot. It was only Mrs Maywell that bothered to answer me.

'Oh she was a strange one, my lovely,' she said, breathing porter fumes into my face as she leaned in closer. 'Not the usual sort. Didn't fit in. Was a disappointment in the end.'

'She was sacked?' I said.

'She wasn't suitable,' Mrs Appleyard said. She gathered up the cards from the abandoned game and began to put them back in their box. 'But you mustn't worry about that. You'll fit in better, won't you my dear?'

I reached for my coat. Felt absurdly disloyal to An, all of a sudden. These are small town people and I am a city girl – for them, being 'suitable' is a case of fitting in, and if Anouk didn't fit in, no matter how hard she tried, then it isn't likely I ever will either.

'I'd better be going. Miss Liversall will wonder where I've got to, and she locks up in an hour,' I said, rather stiffly, and left.

I miss you.
Brix-and-Mortar x x

Plunge Hill: A Case Study

❧   ❧   ❧

Anouk's diary, 17th March 1971. Liversall collection.

It is late – just past 3:30AM. I am awake as I have found
something. While turning over in my sleep I felt something
prickling at my cheek. I tried to brush it away from me,
and then, finding if was something which was inside my
pillowcase, sat up and retrieved it. It is a photograph,
creased and washed out – I suspect it has been through
the laundry more than once – but the colour image it
shows still visible: a young woman, smiling, she is wearing
a striped shirt – cornflower blue and yellow. And, on the
back, written in pen is a name I cannot quite make out, all
but worn away as it is. It looks like it may begin with a M
or perhaps an H or a N. It is hard for me to say.

❧   ❧   ❧

Handwritten note. Foolscap paper. Condition: poor.
Envelope missing. Dated 20th October 1971. Liversall
collection.

J.M. McVulpin

Dear Maurice,

I had another dream last night. You were standing in Miss Liversall's kitchen, wet through – your hair dripping. I said something about not making puddles on her floor, and you laughed, and there was something in my hands – a towel perhaps, to dry you off – and I held it up and said, 'I didn't mean it,' or something like that, that made no sense, the way that nightmares never do. I woke up then, standing shivering in the dark in the middle of my bedroom with my pillow in my hands.

Maybe reading An's entry about finding the photograph in her pillow found its way into my dream. It looks like the both of us have trouble sleeping in this lonely, dismal little room. I am bloody snowed under at work too, which doesn't help. Mrs Chapcott dropped a whole heap of notes to type up into my in-tray today.

'Do these first,' she said – clearly not happy about it. 'These are Dr Kapoor's notes. You'll get used to his handwriting. And pass them back to me directly when they're done, all right?'

I nodded at her and just rolled the paper into my typewriter. She hates Dr Kapoor, you know. When she gave me the notes she had a look on her face like she'd just smelled something bad. I remembered what Anouk said about him – *bad weather* – almost as if she was giving me, who she'd never met and couldn't know would end up sleeping in her bed and reading her diary – a warning. Bad weather. I didn't say anything. We're supposed to pretend we don't understand what we're typing – that we're almost above taking a personal interest. The notes were something to do with blood-typing; there were tables full of numbers and letters that I think were referring to amounts, or were a code for places where the blood has been kept. The case study patient was referred to as H, just as An said.

It was dark again in the hospital today: the corridors all gloomy. It makes people whisper when they're moving around the building. Blackheath was in a bad mood. The power cuts cause extra work for him because he needs to tend to the generators and it aggravates his rotator cuff. I will try to be kind to him. Are you getting the power cuts too? I am so tired. Sometimes I hear the sound the typewriters make when I'm trying to fall asleep. Hailstones. Or someone throwing pennies at the window. The sound – a hard pattering – bends and flows around itself as I become more drowsy and when I am about to drop off it resolves itself into a voice.

We're not happy with your explanation Bridget, can you go over it again? the voice says. *Just start from the beginning and tell me exactly what happened.* It's a man's voice. Not Dad. *In your own words Bridget. Take your time.*

Perhaps I should speak to a doctor. But I don't think it would help. I just need more fresh air. More time to get used to things.

Love,
Bricks-in-The-Wall

ॐ   ॐ   ॐ

Anouk's diary, 18th March 1971. Liversall collection.

I am on my lunch break. Today I am practising my English at my desk rather than in the canteen. Dr Kapoor tells me I am very good. He said so this morning when reading through some of his notes which I had typed up. When I came into work I found him walking back and forth around the typing room, his notes in one hand, the other clamped over his mouth as he read, a deep frown across his forehead. He did this as I took off my coat, hat and gloves and hung them up, as I sat at my desk and began my typing – Dr Kapoor had evidently worked late into the evening, making copious notes as he did so, a fresh untidy pile of which were on one corner of my desk – and as the other typists slowly appeared at their desks and began working. I could see they were all amused by this scenario, anticipating a telling-off for Anouk: had I mistyped a difficult word, got some of the pages in the wrong order, or missed out some crucial information, all with disastrous effect on Dr Kapoor's research? Had I made an error that had cost a life? Truly, these girls do not like me. I worked away, trying not to stare at him wandering around slowly in front of me.

The notes I was presently typing up concerned something called H. All the notes I type up seem to concern H. What is H? I do not know, but it is very important to Dr Kapoor. So far as I can tell from his notes, everything he does seems to revolve around this H: monitoring how H reacts, neurotically measuring H, speculating what may or may not be rejected by H. I pictured a petri dish with a large H painted on its lid. I was knocked out of my thoughts when he clapped the notes shut and looked up.

'Excellent, Anouk,' he said. He sounded happy. 'You've managed to decipher my handwriting. Most impressive.' He stared at me then, for longer than I liked, or so it

37

seemed to me. Then he said, 'Good morning to you.' And with that off he went, back into his surgery.

I got some unpleasant looks from the others after his words of compliment and later, when I asked if anyone would like a cup of tea or coffee, they were silent. I had thought, when I came to England, that I would become English, that it would happen simply because I wanted to be and I would be welcomed for this wanting. Things did not turn out well for me in Newcastle, but here I thought I would have a chance to start again. But it seems starting again is not up to me; it is up to those like the other typists who were born here.

There are two other things which I find I am eager to get down on paper. The first is this: a little after 11 o'clock, a porter appeared, wheeling a trolley on which were loaded candles, a great many of them, each in a little dish. He went from desk to desk, placing one on each corner along with a book of matches. The other women said nothing, or said simply, 'Thank you, Blackheath.' When he reached my desk at the back of the room I asked him, 'What is this for?'

He stared at me for a moment. Like almost everyone here other than my typists, he was a strange old man with white hair and thick glasses. 'Oh,' he said, 'we're due a power cut.'

'A power… cut?' I said.

'Aye,' he said, then, putting together my blank face and my accent, 'it's when they turn off all the electricity.'

'Who does this? Who turns off our electricity?' I thought of Miss Liversall with her insistence on lights being out by 8pm.

'Well, the government, I suppose.'

'Why do they do that?' I asked. I could hear some of the other typists laughing. I suppose I sounded rather absurd. Bless my porter though, he was kind.

'There's not enough of it,' he said, trying to sound authoritative. 'Unions and Ted Heath and… all that.'

'For how long will this last?' I asked. 'When does it begin?'

'Sometime this afternoon,' he said. 'You've a little while yet.' Then he trundled his trolley away, the sound of its squeaky wheels disappearing down a corridor.

So this is what happens here? The electricity is simply stopped and life is expected to go on? I continued working, typing away at Dr Kapoor's notes, but I couldn't help looking up at the lights, worrying that they would at any moment turn off and leave the room in darkness. I wanted to ask someone: what about the machinery? I have vaguely presumed that beyond the door through which Dr Kapoor disappears every morning there are monitors, instruments, scanners: things which keep people alive and require electricity. This is a hospital after all. But when I stopped my typing and looked first at my little candle and then at the other women, hoping for some kind of reassurance, they simply smirked and exchanged glances with one another. I can see that they are aware of my concern, my anxiety, but they do not care – they find it funny.

This brings me onto my second curious thing. I returned to typing up Kapoor's notes. No matter, I thought. Let them cut the power, if this is how things are done here. A few minutes passed. Then I noticed something: a noise, a rattling. It was the sound of my candle clinking in its little dish. All the other girls' candles in all their dishes also began clinking, the noise growing louder, more insistent. I felt my desk begin to vibrate, my chair, the floor beneath it. I looked round at the other women. They were ignoring it, pretending it wasn't happening, simply staring ahead of themselves, their hands frozen in place on their typewriter keys, but not typing, simply holding them in place, their fringes quivering with the rumbling. I felt quite seized by panic as it swelled around us, shaking the walls, but before I could stand or cry out, it quite suddenly stopped, dropping from the room and shrinking to nothing. There was a brief moment of silence and then the women all resumed their typing.[7]

I have overrun my lunch hour with this diary. It has not gone unnoticed. Even as I write I am aware of the others looking over their shoulders at me, wondering what I am writing. I shall hide you from them, notebook.

---

7 This is really fascinating. Not only a visual and auditory hallucination, but a kinetic one to boot. I'm not aware of finding these anywhere else in the medical literature. Bridget is here, of course, projecting her own symptoms onto her invented alter ego, Anouk (AN for Anonymous – how sneaky a sickening mind can become!) but we can assume the substance of this experience – the hallucination of some kind of tremor or earthquake – was her own. How strange it is, as I collate her papers into some kind of sense, to read of her impression of the building trembling around her, as around me the bustle of the removals men echoes up through the stairwells and into my office. There are white vans outside. The trust is reallocating the medical equipment, and I suspect what cannot be used elsewhere will be sold or abandoned. As I peer out of my window I see someone – perhaps Chapcott – out on the front lawn remonstrating with the workmen. Her hands move through the air jaggedly: the woman has always been highly strung. I press my hand against the window, for the moment, my papers almost forgotten. I could go down there. Could offer her some words of comfort. *Plunge Hill will rise again.* A door nearby slams and there's a high-pitched metallic scrape as something – possibly a filing cabinet – is dragged out of an office. I return to these papers, and Bridget, and her wild fantasies. There's no time to waste.

J.M. McVulpin

❧ ❧ ❧

Letter, typed. Envelope addressed to Mr and Mrs Shipley, 245 Acadia Place, London. Envelope is stamped and postmarked 22nd October 1971 and has been opened neatly with a letter opener. Condition: excellent. Shipley Collection.

Dear Mum and Dad,

I am fine. That's the first thing. Really thriving, actually. I really think if you were to see me now you wouldn't even recognise me. Things have improved for me such a lot. I'm sleeping much better and eating well. No more nightmares. I've put some weight back on – but not too much – and I am even making a few friends, too!

There's one girl I've been palling around with – An, she's called – and I think you'd really like her. We have lunch together most days, sitting in the canteen at the hospital when it's quiet, and walking around a bit in the grounds when it's not. An has a boyfriend, Clive, and when he's around he takes us out to Manchester in his car. He always brings presents for me as well as her, so I don't feel left out. Isn't that decent of him? Last time it was a box of Black Magic. Yum! An and I have been chosen to do the administrative work on a special case study. I can't say too much about it – medical confidentiality and all that – but I think if you could see us here at our desks, typing away together, you'd both be really impressed.

I know things weren't the best, last year, but I feel much better now and we are still family and it would be lovely to hear from you – just a line – if you have time.

Your daughter,
Bridget.

⁂ ⁂ ⁂

Anouk's diary, 20th March 1971. Liversall collection.

Although it is Saturday – the weekend – the typists must work. We are allowed to have Sundays to ourselves, but Dr Kapoor's missives demand attention six days a week. My letter, the one which brought me here, did not state this was to be the case but it was made clear to me by Mrs Chapcott yesterday. Nonetheless, I have received my first pay packet from the hospital. It is not much – Miss Liversall receives a large percentage directly. Nonetheless, I decided I would go to the pub. As we were leaving the hospital I thought *Vad i helvete!* and asked the other typists if they wanted to come with me but they said no.

So, I am here, drinking an orange juice alone. The only drink they seem to sell here is something called Plunge Porter, presumably a local beer. It is dark and has the consistency of muddy puddles. I have bought my English thesaurus so I can learn new words like *missive* and *percentage* (I use the photograph I found in my pillowcase as a bookmark, the picture of happy-looking M or H or N) and have sat by the window so I can look out at the village green which makes up the centre of Plunge Hill. For all my feelings of wrongness about this place, it has beauty: the laburnums which grow around the pub seem to be permanently in bloom.

I am alone, as I said, but not quite alone. I arrived just after five o'clock and there was a group of old people at the far end of the bar, wreathed in cigarette smoke. I could tell from the empty glasses that surrounded them and the volume of their conversation that they had already been here a while. They fell quiet as I approached the bar, ordered my drink and sat down at my table. But then they resumed their fun, laughing, sometimes slapping one another, at other times breaking into brief songs – at one point I thought them to all be weeping.

They are singing now, some folk song, a murder ballad in which one of the men, a grey-haired old man, sings the words with everyone else joining on a repeated refrain. It is so strange. I shall write down some of it.

Then twixt my two girls I was forced to choose
Which of them it was time to lose.
Hoo-wee wash and wail.
Shake hands with the devil, don't pull him by the tail.
The nagging shrew who give me grief
Or my sharp mistress who sleep in her sheath.
Hoo-wee wash and wail.
Shake hands with the devil, don't pull him by the tail.
I went down to the well and drank my stout.
Then went home and let the two have it out.
Hoo-wee wash and wail.
Shake hands with the devil, don't pull him by the tail.
Happy you may find the man with a wife
But joy is for he with blood on his knife.
Hoo-wee wash and wail.
Shake hands with the devil, don't pull him by the tail.

And that is that. They applauded the one who led the singing and have now filed outside. One gets a measure of the strangeness of a place when you see its people drunk. I had seen such things in Uppsala and in Newcastle. I certainly saw much strangeness with Clive, who drank.

Curiously, this song about a knife which is also a lover has reminded me of an occurrence at my work, or rather it has made me realise that this morning there was an occurrence. I was typing away as usual: *10:13am: administered H a half gill of blood extracted from sus scrofa. End results for H remain inconclusive but she did not react well. Could be necessary to confect basophil inhibitor...*

Not so different from the usual notes I am required to type up for Dr Kapoor. But something stands out, something which snagged in my mind and which has only just come to the fore: that *she*.

It surprised me. I had thought of H as a petri dish. Perhaps the code for a certain type of experiment. At best, I imagined poor H as a rabbit or rat or some other unfortunate creature subject to Kapoor's unholy investigations. But there it was. That *she*. So am I to conclude that H is a person? Is Dr Kapoor treating a patient? And if so, what is he doing to her? It sounds less like treatment and more like experiments. Does he only treat the one pat

I had to stop my writing just now. As I was scribbling away there was a loud slam at the window alongside my table that caused me to jump. I saw, fleetingly, the palm of a hand slapping against the glass and then retreating, but the hand was up high, causing the hanging basket to swing. I knocked over my drink as I stood up to back away. The orange puddle crept across the table towards my diary and dripped onto to the floor. I went to the bar to get a towel and when I returned I peered out and saw them, my old people.

They are still there now, out on the village green, shouting and cheering, very drunk. Some are perched on top of the shoulders of the others as they are taking turns running at one another, trying to knock each other off. I see others joining them, a crowd forming, some cheering them on, others also grappling onto one another's shoulders to join in. Many of them seem to look at me, stopped momentarily in their tracks, as though they dislike to see me here. I suppose I spoil their fun by not being a part of it, by being an outsider. Among them are some faces I recognise: old people I've seen here and there around town, the man who was singing, the little white-haired lady from the hospital shop, the porter – Blackheath, they call him – who cleans the hospital and brings round the candles. But it is unsettling to see them, so old and so active. It is an unsettling combination, as though they are children made up to look like seniors.

It is getting dark. Of course, there are no streetlights in Plunge Hill. I shall stop writing now and see if I can slip out quietly and go to Miss Liversall's house.

※　※　※

Letter, handwritten. Envelope postmarked 1st November 1971. Shipley collection.

Maurice,

Pinch and a punch for the first of the month, little one!

Strangest thing happened tonight. I got in and Miss Liversall was arguing with somebody in the kitchen. My head was full of thoughts about An – about Clive, about her strange paranoia – I am beginning to see what they meant when they said she wasn't suitable – and the funny mood I was in might have coloured the way I heard what they were saying. But all the same, I am pretty sure they were fighting about me.

'It's excessive,' Miss Liversall was saying, in that high-pitched, wheedling little voice she has. 'An utter indulgence. The hospital pays an allowance for her food and that's more than sufficient.'

'Now Hilda,' the voice – I recognised it as Mrs Maywell's – 'it does no harm, does it? To make her feel at home?'

'I don't see why…'

'If you don't shape up your ideas, she'll let us down – like the other one – and then where will we be…?'

'I hope you're not blaming me for that!' Liversall said. I heard a cupboard door slam. 'It wasn't *my* fault. I did exactly as Kapoor asked me to. If there's anyone to blame—'

'The man is doing his best, Hilda. And while he does it, a bit of friendliness wouldn't cost you anything. And I've got all this lamb – a freezer full of it. Parag keeps bringing it to the house and somebody's got to eat it.'

'You try being friendly with one in the house. You know the sort Chapcott picks. *If the hospital's got to have one, we may as well make it a bad one* – that's what she says. But I'm the one who has to wash their bed sheets.'

'It's only a pie. Calm yourself.'

'It's an imposition, is what it is. I keep a nice house. And to have to open it up for the likes of—'

'You're doing your bit. For all of us.' Mrs Maywell's voice was soft. Wheedling. 'We're all really grateful. And you're doing it for yourself too, aren't you? That hip of yours—'

'Don't soft-soap me, Ada. I don't see you queuing up to take them in…'

They must have heard me in the hall, taking off my coat, because they stopped talking and their faces appeared around the kitchen door – Liversall looking all sulky, wringing a tea towel between her fists, and Mrs Maywell smiling at me. She had a covered dish in her hands.

'I've brought a pie, my lovely,' she said. 'It's lamb. Bowland lamb. Couldn't get more local. Too much for me – I'd never eat it all on my own. So I thought I'd just pop it around here and—'

'You'll be going, I expect,' Liversall said, as if I wasn't standing there. 'The nights are drawing in. You don't want to let the cold get onto that chest of yours, do you, Ada?'

Mrs Maywell put the dish down on the sideboard, coughing a little, nodded at me, and left. I could tell from the start that Miss Liversall and I were never really going to be friends, but all that fuss over a bloody pie.

Oh, I won't moan any more. I'm going to get into bed and read An's diary now. Just a page or two night by night, trying to make it – to make *her* – last. She is the best friend I've got here. Maybe they really were picking on her, you know – the drab birds. And I don't think they like me much either. Am I the 'bad one' they were talking about? Is that what they all think of me?

Wrap up warm.
X X X X Wheat-a-Brix.

ક૬   ક૬   ક૬

Anouk's diary, 22nd March 1971. Liversall Collection.

This morning something [illegible]
   This morning I [illegible]
   [illegible]
   [illegible]
   Bastard! Shit! *Knull!* Look at my handwriting. I must calm myself. Anouk, you are alone. You are on a bus. The bus is all but empty, just you and the driver. You are safe. You are alone.

There. That is better. My hand is steadier.

This morning something upsetting took place. I do not know quite how to write about it.

This morning as I was passing through the village green on my way to the bus stop I stopped, hearing noise and movement. I looked around but I was alone. The green is a wide open space and I was the only one present, there could be no doubt. But then came the noise again: a sort of groaning accompanied by a rattle. It was coming from within a shrubbery. I realised with a shock that there indeed was a figure alongside me, a man who was prostate through the branches, neither on top of them nor on the ground, suspended within its branches where, presumably, he had fallen.

'*Jarvlata!*' I shouted instinctively, then, 'Oh, goodness me!' My first thought was that he had been assaulted and knocked into here and had received perhaps a blow on the head, and so I immediately began to try to help him, parting the bushes, such as I could, pulling at his hand and saying, 'Come on, come on.' But as I did this I then smelled the alcohol and began to suspect that he had in fact fallen in here, no doubt following similar revelries to those I had witnessed at The Red Pony on Saturday. I recognised the thick glasses and the white hair spilling over the twigs to be that of my porter, the man who had brought a candle for me and been kind. He seemed still unconscious, and yet he also groaned and complied as I reached into the bush and pulled at his other hand, sitting up, his eyes opening.

'Here we go,' I said. He lifted his arms, finally prising himself free of the bush. An arm remained idle in the air as he dropped into a sitting position in the path.

'Thank you, thank you,' he replied, his eyes half closed. The arm dropped and he rubbed his forehead. Then he looked at me, and something seemed to drop out of him, waking him up, all self-pity replaced by something I could not quite understand, something harder. For a moment he seemed most moved to see me, as though he might start crying.

'You?' he said. 'It's you.' He laughed at this, but it was a laugh not of humour, but of anxiety, bitterness. 'Doesn't that just take the biscuit... *You.*'

'Me?' I said. 'But what is wrong with me?'

Anger then, propelling him upwards, flailing as he stood 'That's just it! That's just it!' he shouted. He took as a step or two away from me, as though to leave, but then rounded, pointing a finger at me. 'Just the right thing is wrong with you. You know, you come across all...' he gestured me up and down, his mouth snarled, 'all... *nice.* All normal. But do you know what, you deserve it. Your lot always do. There's always something, always someone, always a Clive, *shit*—' His mouth snapped shut on that last syllable, pursed, his eyes suddenly on the defensive, watching me. He had said too much.

I'm not sure what the words are which would describe how I felt at hearing Clive's name. It was a feeling as though a glass pane had shattered suddenly close by, but the sound of that shattering was somehow prolonged, drawn out like a note on a violin, and everywhere: in the trees, in the ground, in the sky.

I spoke slowly: 'What do you know about Clive?'

'I…it's…' He searched the horizon, licking his lips, thinking of a way he could unsay that name. 'I'm sorry, love. I'm drunk. You know how it is. Talking shite.'

'It is not this *shite*,' I said. 'You will tell me what you know.'

He seemed to nod then. There was a long pause, filled with breeze and birdsong. 'Yeah,' he said. 'Aye, alright – we know about Clive.' He tilted his head, his hair swinging out, as though he were about to acquiesce further, to level with me.

Then he sprang forward, lunging at me, the flats of his fingertips connecting with my breasts. It was not a violent push but enough to upend me. I landed on the gravel path, twisting awkwardly as I fell. By the time I had righted myself I was again alone, my porter a fleeting billow of dust and grit.

I had been calm when speaking to him, or had affected as much, but it came to me now: shaking and tears, fretting and rocking. That shattering glass sound rushing in at me. *Clive.* Can he know what I did?

I feel the shakes coming on again. I can hear the first of the girls coming in, their light voices at the door.

Oh no, oh no, oh no. *Å nej, nej, nej nej nej nej nej.*

❧ ❧ ❧

Letter, typed. Envelope intact, stamped and postmarked 6th November 1971. Condition: excellent. Shipley collection.

Dear Mum and Dad,

PLEASE read this letter right the way through to the end. Don't throw it away. PLEASE. It's important.

I'm not supposed to tell you this, I don't think. But something happened and I think you'll want to know about it. I'll start from the beginning. Mrs Chapcott sent me down to the incinerator with a box of patient records that needed to be destroyed. I supposed they were notes from patients that had died. It was a sad thought – the sense of failure, I suppose – all these people that the doctors couldn't help anymore, and I tried not to dwell on it as I trotted along the corridor in the dark with my candle making wobbly shadows up the walls. Dr Kapoor, the man I am typing for, has an office down here. The door was open and as I came past with my candle and my box of papers he called me in.

He was sitting there at his desk, surrounded by candles of his own: stuck onto the covers of hardbacked books and medical journals, along the top of the radiator in glass jars and bottles, even a couple on the floor sticking out of old teacups.

'Yes, Dr Kapoor?'

He looked like he'd seen a ghost, gasped, then just as quickly gathered himself.

'I'm sorry,' he said. 'You must forgive me. I thought you were Anouk. My previous typist. When you came in – your hair – I thought that you were she.'

'Anouk isn't here anymore,' I said. 'She left. I've been doing your typing.'

(Mum, Dad – I'll explain about that in a bit, all right?[8] The most important thing is, whatever I've said before, that Anouk was here – she really was here, in the hospital, at my desk, sleeping in my room – and now she's not, all right? I'll tell you the rest later. In person. Just READ THIS.)

He squinted at me through the jumping shadows and yellow candlelight.

'You were written to? Chapcott wrote to offer you her position?'

'Yes, Dr Kapoor.'

He looked at me carefully, rubbed his chin and sighed.

'I wish she wouldn't…' his voice tailed away.

'Wouldn't what?'

'It doesn't matter. Chapcott supervises the typists. Maywell operates the canteen. Blackheath oversees our minor practical matters. Liversall provides hospitality. And I… I have my own work. We all have our parts to play.'[9]

---

8   Oh Bridget. What a tangled web we weave…

9   I feel the urge to note the part I myself play and the work I do in attending to the emotional, mental, behavioural and even spiritual health of the residents of Plunge Hill village and the surrounding scattered hamlets and farms. Ego? Certainly. I am but human, and all physicians carry their own wounds. How could it be otherwise? Psychiatry is not a glamorous speciality: I do understand that. We are apt to be overlooked. Forgotten. My father regularly expressed a disappoint-

'Yes,' I said, slowly. 'All doing our bit. I've been typing up your notes, Dr Kapoor. I hope they've been satisfactory.'

'Never underestimate the importance of your role, my dear. The typing pool is the lifeblood of Plunge Hill itself. And you are a part of it. Though I have to say my work has been progressing in a much less satisfactory fashion than your own.'

'With Patient H?' I said. He looked up sharply.

'Yes. H has a most rare condition. She hungers and wastes and I cannot find the thing she needs. What has caused this? I do not know. For now, it is more important for me to find a solution. And time dwindles, Miss Shipley. It

---

ment that I did not choose surgery. I did not tell him – I rarely tell anyone – that I cannot stand the sight of blood. But it is a truth (and one I plan to research more fully with a study in respect of which I am currently awaiting news of a grant application) that the residents of these damp hills and dark valleys suffer from a luxuriant and abundant range of mental infirmities. All pathology is here: the sociopath, the obsessive, the nymphomaniac, the depressive, the psychotic. The landscape itself feeds these mental maladies, I believe, and my duty here is to tend to them, as a shepherd tends his lambs. That is the part I play. You'd be surprised at how many of my colleagues I treat. Though never Parag Kapoor. Never Chapcott (her first name is Marie – though she has never allowed me to use it). You must – however poor Bridget chooses to represent them in these pages, and whatever stories the press may go on to publish about them and their work in the months and years to come – you must believe that my colleagues were professionals until the very end. As I am. I will be the last to leave this place, I think.

dwindles. December will be upon us before we know it. H's condition is unpredictable. Its peculiar effects seem to...' he scratched the back of his neck with a pencil, 'radiate.'

'She's contagious?'

'After a fashion... but these effects. They are not entirely unwelcome to those who suffer from them. Suffer is the wrong word.' He scratched his head. 'Unprecedented effects. Welcome effects. Which is part of the problem.'

'I'm not sure I...'

He shook his head. 'It doesn't matter. Sometimes in the cause of the problem we can find its solution, and looking back can assist us in going forwards, but at other times—'

'Will she die, this patient of yours?' I asked.

'I don't think so, Miss Shipley. I think it will be worse than that.'

He smiled, and adjusted his tie, and motioned for me to sit down.

'Let us look forward. That's what I say. This patient of mine, Miss Shipley, she matters. If I can get her back to full health – back to former vitality – well then, many others will benefit from this.'

'You can give the treatment to others with her disease?'

'After a fashion, yes. And do you know,' he leaned forward, his eyes alight with the glow from the candle, 'the knock-on effects of this cannot be underestimated. Would you laugh,' he looked at me kindly, 'yes, I think you probably would laugh – if I told you that here at Plunge Hill Hospital we may even be looking to cure death itself. What do you think of that?' he leaned back in his chair. 'You will think I have let the long working hours and stress of my job addle my mind. But…'

He went on a bit here, Mum. *No more suffering*, he said. *Nobody will ever need to languish in a hospital bed again*, he said. That was the gist of it. I know what you're thinking. I thought exactly the same thing. Maurice. This could be a real chance for him, couldn't it?

'There's a long way to go before the results are certain,' he smiled, his stethoscope – which was around his neck – glinting in the candlelight, and his eyes darting around the room as if all the grateful patients he was imagining were really in there with us, standing around us in their white gowns like a choir. 'And as I said, the work is not going well. But I have hope. I still have hope, dear Bridget – if I may – that the price we might pay for our breakthrough might be less than we thought. We've always used animals, you know. The first blood transfusions. The first transplants. Then human patients – criminals, mainly – paying off their debt to society by giving the use of their bodies to the medical profession. But thanks to those sacrifices we know more now. Our treatments are more humane. We can have hope. And you, you most of all of us, must hope with me. Can you do that?' he spoke urgently – almost as if he was preaching from a pulpit, rather than just chatting to me across his dimly lit desk.

'I'm working as well as I can, Sir,' I said.

'Of course. And you must work harder. We both must.'

Can I tell him about Maurice, Mum? Can I ask him if he'd be all right with you and Dad bringing Maurice up here?

Your loving daughter,
Bridget

Editor's note

I find I am inclined to intrude on the narrative to compose a few words on the topic of empathy. Knowing as I do that much of what Bridget Shipley relays is coloured by her pathology – indeed a great deal is entirely fabricated – I struggle to feel any sympathy for her evident anxiety. I read her pleas to her parents, her frankly pathetic missives to her unresponsive brother, her disquieting creation 'Anouk', and I find them so naked in their desperation for some form of human contact – for some form of attention – that I am, rather ashamed though I am to admit it, repelled. My own response is simply one of abreactive dismissal. *Stupid girl*, I find myself thinking. *You stupid, stupid girl.*

It should go without saying that I consider this something of a serious professional failing on my part. The work of a psychiatrist is one of empathy, nothing more. Measured, studiously considered and skilfully applied empathy. One must be able to feel one's way around the mind of one's subject, appreciating the structure one finds which allows for the unique composition of thought, familiarising oneself with the psychic ley-lines, sitting in their thinking much like an attentive motorist in the passenger seat, observing their reactions and manoeuvres and experiencing them as though they were one's own.

And so I have removed myself from my office, taking with me my typewriter and my boxes of documents, and have come to the hospital's typing pool. Or former hospital's typing pool, as I suppose I should get used to thinking about Plunge Hill. I am typing this whilst sat at the desk at the rear of the room – Bridget's desk, the scene of much of her unravelling – ahead of me the long, dark staircase leading to the gardens on one side, the double doors into the body of the hospital on the other. Although it is very much deserted here, I close my eyes and imagine the place bustling with activity and noise: the din of the typewriters, the chatter of the girls, the warmth of so many bodies. And I begin to imagine I am Bridget Shipley: I have her hopes, her fears, her complicated anxieties, I have her parents, have Maurice as my brother, Anouk as my imaginary friend.

Sadly, reality intrudes most abruptly. The swing doors burst open and two of the removal men march in, pulling along with them a trolley, and begin dragging one of the filing cabinet units alongside me out of its place. Ordinarily, I would move on of course, find a desk elsewhere at which I could continue my work. But the typing pool is one of the scant places to be found in the hospital where desks remain serviceable. Elsewhere they are stacked into corners, on their sides or piled high with boxes. It has been made clear to me that my own office – now denuded of its desk, its sofa, its coffee table, its shelving, even its light bulb – is officially off-limits. And so I sit and wait for the two men to finish. It is a noisy process, the metal cabinets scraping the wooden floor, their doors sliding open and shut, the two men shouting all manner of expletives to one another as they try to haul it onto the trolley, oblivious not only to my work but to my presence. I close my eyes.

The commotion gives way quite suddenly to the hushed sound of the filing cabinets, lifted free from the ground, exiting through the swinging doors, the trolley's rubber wheels rolling smoothly away. I open my eyes, ready to resume my work, when I notice that the removal of the filing cabinets has uncovered something. There is a small entrance in the brickwork, a few feet up from the floor and very narrow. I stand up and approach it, peering inside, into the darkness. It is, of course, the bottom of a chute, one built in the original hospital for the purpose of collecting papers dropped from the rooms above the typing pool, a system long abandoned and, for the most part, bricked up. I peer up at the unlit flue. Yes, it is certainly very narrow. A human body would only be able to gain passage through it under the most extreme of circumstances.

Plunge Hill: A Case Study

Anouk's diary, 27th March 1971. Liversall collection.

I am writing this outside, in the sunshine. Inside it is dark. Another power cut. Pitch black, yet I should be in there typing. 'You're all touch typists, aren't you girls?' Chapcott said. She speaks about pulling together, and Blitz spirit, and the end to all their troubles coming very soon – as if she alone is able to predict the end to these power cuts. I could not bear it. Instead I crept away to the far edge of the hospital grounds, where the gardens are separated from the moor only by a thin wire fence meant to keep out the sheep and a small stone surrounded by a circle of flowers. Inscribed into the rock is the number 1827. I know this place: the photographs in the hospital from the Easter Parade show the ladies from the typing pool here, in their best clothes, gathered around the neck of an old well. I have heard of old traditions like this. And now I am perched on the well from the photographs, writing here.

I do not like to be the last to come into the typing room, with so many unfriendly faces watching me, but that is what happened this morning, after my altercation on the village green.

'You're rather late, Anouk,' said Mrs Chapcott.

'Yes,' I said. 'I am sorry. There was an incident.'

They laughed at that, all of them.

'Oh yes?' said Mrs Chapcott.

'It was the porter,' I said. 'The one who brings the candles. He was very drunk. I encountered him in the street on the way here and he was very rude to me and then he assaulted me.'

More laughter. It seemed even Mrs Chapcott could not help herself.

'Oh, you mean Mr Blackheath.'

'Yes,' I said. 'He upset me greatly.'

Yet more laughter, heads turning to exchange glances. Indeed, I felt ridiculous saying all this while removing my coat, hat and gloves, as though such things – items of outdoor clothing and violence – are all one and the same.

'He attacked me,' I told Chapcott. 'He pushed me. Pushed me right to the ground.'

'Anouk,' she said, nothing more. A grin.

'And he said something to me,' I said. I had not entered with a plan but instinctively had wanted to keep this detail – the mention of Clive – to myself. But I was quite unexpectedly unable to stop myself. Suddenly I wanted badly someone to listen to what I told them, to be interested and concerned, to be defensive. I suppose the English word is *friend*. 'He said something about someone

I used to know. He seemed to know about me from the time before I came to Plunge Hill.' I had begun to cry.

The smiles had melted away from the faces around me. After a few seconds of silence they all being to type again, all except Mrs Chapcott.

'Anouk,' she said, standing up, coming over towards me, her voice lowered but calm, a hardness to it. 'Assault is a serious word. I don't know if that's the sort of thing you bandy about where you come from but here it's just not the done thing. Not without proof. I take it you have none?'

'But he pushed me. I was walking past—'

'It's a simple question, Anouk. Proof. Yes or no?'

'Well… no.'

'Then I'm afraid I must say it does sound like you've perhaps overreacted a touch. I've known Mr Blackheath for years and I simply cannot imagine him,' she laughed, 'hurting anyone. I'm sure he was still a little merry from a night in The Pony. But the sort of thing you're talking about, Holly, well it just doesn't happen here.'

'Yes, yes,' I said, shuffling toward my desk. I now wanted this conversation to be over. 'I see.' I sat down.

'Good,' she said, following. 'I'm glad you understand. You are doing well. I know it's difficult when you're trying to fit in to a new place.'

'Holly…' I said.

'I…' she glared at me for second. 'I beg your pardon?'

'My name is Anouk. You called me Holly.'

She gave a small laugh, shaking her head. 'You must be mistaken. I know you struggle with the language but I assure you it is really rather straightforward. Now, today I need you to stop your work on Dr Kapoor's notes and focus on this.' She dropped a file onto my desk.

'Very well,' I said. I picked up the notes and began to type, grateful to have something to distract. Gradually, my altercation with this Mr Blackheath melted into the background, began to seem more and more improbable.

After an hour or so, Dr Kapoor emerged from his surgery and made a beeline for my desk.

'Anouk, good morning. These are for you.' He dumped a handful of notes onto my desk and stuck his hand out towards me, waiting, his usual distracted, distant self. 'May I have my typed-up notes from last night?'

'I'm sorry, Dr Kapoor. I've not yet been able to—'

'Excuse me?'

'I've been working on…' I looked at my notes, 'Dr Woodward's notes.'

'Dr Woodward?' He stared, frowning. 'But why?'

'It's important to get *some* of the work of the hospital done, Dr Kapoor,' said Mrs Chapcott. Tension filled the room: never before have I seen anyone speak to Dr Kapoor with anything less than absolute deference.

There was a moment of silence while Kapoor looked at Mrs Chapcott, then at me, then in a low tone said, 'My work is the work of the hospital, Mrs Chapcott.'

'Yes,' she said pleasantly. 'But I'm afraid it isn't as pressing as Dr Woodward's work.'

'Not as pressing?'

'That's right. I believe using Anouk's time exclusively for your work is unwise, Dr Kapoor.'

'Unwise?'

'Yes, unwise. Don't you agree?'

'Mrs Chapcott,' he leaned back, ran a hand across his forehead, stared upwards, 'I believe I am the doctor here. What is pressing and what is not is decided by myself. You know how urgent my work is.'

I'm not sure why but this last statement caused Mrs Chapcott's mask to slip. 'Yes, but why her?' She gestured at me. 'Of all people.'

'Because you won't give me anyone else to type up my research!' Dr Kapoor banged his knuckles on my desk. The typing around us ceased as the other girls looked over towards us. 'A page here and there, once or twice a week. That's no good – do you understand? You treat my work as though it's some extravagance, all of you, everyone. Am I the only one here who cares for human life?'

'That's enough,' she said.

'None of you care. You're happy so long as you've all got your health—'

He was cut off when the room suddenly turned black.

'Oh, for crying out loud,' said Mrs Chapcott.

'Bloody hell!' I could still see the dark outline of Dr Kapoor – his fringe had fallen across his face. 'Another power cut? Was this scheduled?'

'I don't know,' said Chapcott.

For a moment the room was quiet. The typists remained silent, Dr Kapoor and Mrs Chapcott had ceased arguing, and the hum of hospital machinery had fallen silent. We all listened, waiting to hear the emergency generators kick in.

It was quite a shock when the silence was interrupted by the swing door crashing open as a trolley was wheeled into the room. I heard a few of the girls gasp and then giggle nervously. I couldn't see who was pushing the trolley along, my unpleasant porter or someone else. Although dark he knew the room well enough to navigate it, whoever it was, stopping by each desk to set down a candle. I wondered should I try to smell him, to see if the odour of alcohol would give him away, this Mr Blackheath? But I felt my skin prickle as I heard the figure come to a halt in front of me and the breath stopped in my chest. He clinked down a dish and candle on the corner of my desk, his hand making the slightest brush against mine.

'Mrs Chapcott, I'm just going,' I said, bolting out of my chair, 'just going to get some fresh air.' I swung my handbag over my shoulder, feeling it clatter against an in-tray on one of the desks, and made my way to the exit, the dim light from the hallway at the top of the stairs illuminating my way. When I got to the top I realised I'd brought Dr Kapoor's latest notes with me.

And so here I am, perched on the well in the grounds of the hospital, writing. I should perhaps go back inside now. The power may be back on and in any case did anything so terrible occur? The back of a man's hand brushed against mine, nothing more. Things which alarm us in the dark seem as nothing in the daylight. This day has given me the most tremendous headache. Such anxiety, it muddles my thoughts.

Summary: administered half a gal sample of AB+ to H,
reads the opening of Dr Kapoor's latest notes. *Time of C.D.
no longer than 10 mins prior and yet results no different.*

I think about my photograph girl: M or H or N,
smiling and happy. And I think about Dr Kapoor's words
to Mrs Chapcott, his outrage. *Am I the only one here who
cares for human life?* An odd thing to say. In a hospital
everyone cares for such things – it is the purpose of
the place. Why would he say it unless there were some
disagreement about his methods? Some extravagance, is
that what he said? I find it connected to these notes, to
AB+, a blood type. C.D. I know – or I think I know –
stands for clinical death. I have such a headache, but I
think of Kapoor's late nights in his secret surgery, his notes
and his patient – his H – and, diary, I know this to be a
silly notion, the sort of thing which should seem ludicrous
here, out among the foxgloves and the crocuses, but I think
Dr Kapoor is taking blood from the dead bodies – from
the deceased patients, and also from animals – sheep and
lambs from the countryside around the hospital, when he
can get them, and I think he is using this blood to do
experiments on H, his secret patient, my poor photograph
girl. Is this who H is? Is she

Plunge Hill: A Case Study

❧   ❧   ❧

Letter, typed, with handwritten signatures added at the bottom in black fountain pen ink. Basildon Bond watermarked paper and envelope. Envelope has been ripped open, nearly in half. Letter is torn slightly but perfectly legible. Condition: generally fair with some damage (as described). Dated 9th November 1972. Liversall collection.

Bridget,

We acknowledge your letter. We write only to communicate that we feel it is inappropriate for you to contact us further in light of everything that has happened. Despite our entreaties, the police have decided not to take the matter of last year further. As you know, we have no choice but to respect that decision. You are an adult, and the law has decided you are a free woman, entitled to make your own way in the world without interference. Nevertheless, we cannot in all good conscience continue with you and that is a situation that is not likely to change. We have advised this before, and given the contents of your last letter to us, we will advise you again: please see a doctor. We have enclosed a cheque,[10] which we hope will go some way to

---

10   The cheque remained with the letter, uncashed. It was made out to Miss B. Shipley, for a sum of three hundred pounds. This is the first letter I found in Bridget's room, tucked into her suitcase, which was placed neatly under the diminutive bed she slept in while boarding with Miss Liversall. My visit to Miss Liversall took place mere hours after the discovery of Bridget's body. She was, perhaps, still lying in the long grass, a keening chorus of nurses gathered open-mouthed around her, kneeling to lift her white exsanguinated limbs onto the trolley Mr Blackheath had waiting for her. All this while I smartly rapped – three times – with the mermaid-shaped knocker at Miss Liversall's door. Three hundred pounds! The sum itself, and the ease by which Bridget's parents dispatched it to their estranged daughter – buying her absence from their lives, in effect – tells you everything you need to know about the social and economic background from which our young Bridget came.

I would have seen her as a private patient, of course, if she'd have turned up, cheque in hand, outlining her symptoms – the delusions about a Swedish predecessor, life-saving basement experiments, something to do with the blood. If she'd have confessed about the night terrors that had been troubling her, a leaking out of unexpressed guilt, she would have found me a sympathetic, warm, and most of all, professional listener. I don't often take on private patients – the National Health Service tends to look down on that – but given her background, the fact that her parents were probably more accustomed to private doctors in the leafy North London suburbs than overstretched public clinics, well, I would have made an exception. And I would have had such good advice for her.

Many an evening – this evening, as an example – I sit up late with a single candle burning in a saucer, scratching away at my hand-written

Plunge Hill: A Case Study

enabling you to access the assistance you need, and we trust this will discharge our responsibility to you and so put an end to your communications with us.

Mr and Mrs Shipley

✾   ✾   ✾

notes, and wondering what challenges the morning will bring. And I spend those evening hours arranging Bridget's papers and imagining what advice I would have given to her. Forgive me. Forgive me! I am old and my eyesight grows dim and the marks I make on the paper are not clear to me. Sometimes I warm myself with a little porter while the wind blows outside the hospital and rattles the thin glass windows in their casements. Do I exaggerate a little in my drunkenness? Do I make my own story – as Bridget made hers – into the stuff of gothic nightmares? Of ghost stories told to frighten children?

I had a nanny when I was a young boy, and she was severe. I remember the smell of her apron: soap and yeast. Where was I? The candle sputters. Oh yes. Bridget. Bridget Shipley and her money. I returned the cheque to her parents with a letter, asking them if I could come and visit. If I could ask them some questions about her. I said I was interested in seeing the letters she had sent home. When they replied they enclosed a parcel of postcards, typewritten letters, greetings cards, etc. The letters had been opened and read, and carefully stored. I have them here now, and by night, by candlelight, as the wind roars, I arrange them on my desk, attempting to mosaic Bridget's madness into some kind of sense, and take my notes.

J.M. McVulpin

Another interruption! I am now back at my desk. I was outside, sat at the well, writing the above, my words about H being both my girl in the creased photograph and Dr Kapoor's secret patient, when something interrupted me. The sound of footsteps. Or rather, no, not the sound of footsteps but the sound of another presence, as though someone were approaching me, walking my direction. But I stopped my writing and looked up and there was no-one – I was alone, or seemed to be. My encounter with Blackheath on the green has left me feeling as though I could at any time be being watched.

I realised the noises I could hear which sounded like shuffling were coming from the well, from inside the well. I peered in but of course it was too dark to see anything. No doubt, I thought, it was perhaps a bird or a rat, or perhaps some settling of stones. I do not believe this is a working well – this is not, surely, the place where the water for the hospital comes from. It seems a very old-fashioned thing – the stone it is made of grey and covered with yellow and blue lichens. Ornamental only, perhaps – just a thing for the hospital people to have their photographs taken in front of twice a year.

As I peered the bottom of the well came into relief and I saw that I was wrong: there was water. It was very far down – dark water below in which I could just about make out the outline of my own head and shoulders reflected back at me. I stared at that outline and thought about Clive. I have made my reckoning with what happened to Clive. Everyone has secrets. I chose not to push away what I did to Clive from my thoughts, not to deny it, but simply to live with it as best as I could. Or so I had thought. My encounter with Blackheath has made me realise that I have also been living with something else: fear. Fear of being found out, of being caught.

Not long after I moved in with him in Newcastle, Clive finished work as a lorry man with Middlebrooks under circumstances I never fully understood. He left for a fortnight but returned in under a week. Something happened somewhere in Germany, in some small town he'd stopped off at. Someone – a girl – made some accusations about him and another driver. All nonsense, he said, but her family kicked up a stink about it to the company so they'd been let go to make things go away.

'What does it mean?' I asked him. 'Let go.'

'It means I'm sacked – out of a job.'

He was very upset and I felt very sorry for him. But, he told me, he had something lined up, work on a building site. Some flats were going up in the east of the city and he had a friend, a *mate,* who worked there and had put in a good word for him. Within days he was down there, returning late, covered in dust and paint, drunk most nights. They drank at the site, him and a group of the other men, crates of beer delivered every couple of days. 'Living the dream,' he said. 'Paradise on earth.' When I asked him when he was expecting to be paid he became evasive. Money, when it did show up, was small – a handful of change here and there, an offer to pay for breakfast in a café from time to time. Gradually, it became clear to me that the beer was his payment. I was working in The Jubilee at the time and my money was going straight on rent and heating and bills.

'You need to be making more money,' I told him one night. 'There must be jobs out there.' He didn't like that. I was facing away from him, drawing the curtains, and got a smack across the back of my head – more a pawing at my hair – which made me turn around, half smiling, not knowing what he was doing. That was when he punched me, his fingers landing square on my face, between the eyes. Further blows followed. I wasn't sure how many, as I passed out. When I came to it was the middle of the night. He'd removed my clothes, laid me in bed and fallen asleep alongside me. A crust of blood adhered my face to the pillow and I could feel something slick and cold across my chest and neck. We joked about it in the morning – I was disgusted, but kept my disgusting secret. I was inexperienced and believed him when he told me that this was what men, especially men who have had too much to drink, are like. Perhaps to wake up like this – aching and nauseous and full of shame from being used by him in my sleep – was nothing at all.

'Sorry, love,' he said. 'You know what happens when a bloke has a few jars.'

It was a few days later when he told me first thing in the morning to come down to the building site after I'd finished my afternoon shift. I'd moved on to Bourgones by the time, a pub with a solicitors' office upstairs. After my afternoon shifts I'd usually go up to the offices to spend an hour or so cleaning up for 'a few bob'. I told Clive as much.

'You can afford to give it a miss this once,' he said, pulling his sweater on with a puff of cement dust. 'I've something I want to show you.'

'Something you want to show me? At the site?'

'Aye,' he said. He was smiling. 'I've a feeling it could be the making of us.'

'Oh,' I said. I knew Clive and the other builders had just finished digging out the basements. I pictured some archaeological discovery, some rare and valuable specimen. We would sell it to the British Museum for a million pounds.

'See you then,' he said.

I was replaying all of this whilst I gazed down into the well. Then I felt as though there was something beneath the water and my reflection: an eye, a large solitary eye, unblinking, watching me. But here is the curious thing. I felt my headache being driven away, as though repelled by some magnetic force. And it was replaced with a feeling that I can only describe as sweetness – a feeling of airiness and freshness and peacefulness flowing through me. Although pleasant, I felt uneasy. I stepped away, to go back into the hospital.

❦   ❦   ❦

Letter, handwritten. Dated 9th November 1972. Liversall Collection.

Plunge Hill: A Case Study

Dear Maurice,

Sometimes I sit in my bedroom at night and chatter away to the lampshade hanging from the ceiling over my bed. I pretend An can hear me and that we're real friends, instead of just imaginary ones. Sometimes I talk to my pillow. Sometimes to the curtains.[11] I do it because I am lonely,

---

11   It is not surprising that, after such a family trauma, and so lately separated from her parents – this is the first time Bridget has lived away from home, remember – she would resort to the use of a transitional object. We think of these as a device of children – the stuffed bear, the tattered comfort blanket, the brightly coloured rattle – but many people I have worked with have had their little talismans to act as a bridge between the haven of home and the rough and tumble of the unknown adult world. Consider Miss R, who would go nowhere without a particular pink handkerchief tucked into her brassiere. Or Mr S, who, on forgetting his lucky keyring, turned around on his journey to work and went home to retrieve it, even though the delay in his journey made him significantly late for an important meeting. Miss R and Mr S were not patients of mine, dear subscriber! No! they are friends – professionals at this very hospital. We all have our little tokens and trinkets that we use to stave off the dark. As I say so often to patients, it isn't the act or the object itself that indicates madness, it is only a matter of degree. I myself have a little picture of Nanny in a fold-up frame in the top drawer of my desk. The frame is silver, heavily embossed, and quite tarnished with age. I rarely open up the frame so I can see Nanny's magnificent, fearsome face, for the sight of her is not necessary. Just holding the frame in my hands and rubbing my thumbs across its embossed surface is enough, most of the time, to calm me and cure me from whatever unwise course of action has suddenly gripped my psyche.

of course, but also because the dreams have got bad – very bad. Last night I was standing on the bank of a great lake or inland sea. The light was strange: it was quite dark, and yet I could see a long way across the water – well enough to see that there was something in the water, some – I don't know – some great thing, and it was swimming towards me, rippling its way through the dark water. And I was standing by the edge waiting for it. I woke up before I could get a good look at it. Before it came to get me. Talking to myself is the way I put off sleep for as long as I can.

'What happened to you, Anouk?' I say. 'Did you get away to Sweden? Back home? Did you find Clive and make it up with him?'

I've never had a boyfriend before. My school was a girls' school, and out of school there was hockey club, and the horse riding – but there were no boys there to be interested in either. I'd sort of hoped that coming here there would be… I don't know. A junior doctor. Or even a pharmacist. But, and I'm only noticing it now I'm sitting here and thinking about it, there's nobody here my age other than the typists. Kapoor must be in his sixties, though it is difficult to tell. Chapcott the same. The Canasta Club all ancient – as old as the hills, which

is their little saying. Nobody my age to take me out to
the cinema.

'What was it like, having a boyfriend, An?' I ask.
'Because it sounds horrible. Was he always that nasty to
you?'

Poor thing. No wonder she was suspicious when she
got here. That she found it hard to make friends.

'I'd have been your friend, An,' I say.

An says nothing, of course. It's funny to think of her
being here, right in this room, only a few months ago.
Sitting here on this bed writing her mad little theories
about Kapoor in her diary while I was back at home in
London.

'What were you up to, Anouk?' I say. 'Was it Miss
Liversall? Did she drive you round the bend?'

It was a sad time for our family then, wasn't it
Maurice? The house was so quiet. People coming and
going, bringing food sometimes. Cards. I stayed in my
room most of the time. Parts of it come back in my
dreams. The things I heard when Mum and Dad were
downstairs arguing late at night – mainly about me. 'You
must try to remember, Bridget,' someone says – a doctor,
I think, showing me the shiny face of an old-fashioned
pocket watch and trying to send me to sleep. Is that why

I don't remember things very well? Did a doctor back in London scramble my head?

Hello Anouk. Are you out there somewhere? Did you know I was coming? Did you leave your diary for me? I think you did, which is why I don't feel a bit guilty about reading it. Maybe I'll have a dream about you tonight instead. In my dream you'll run away back to Newcastle to meet Clive in the Jubilee. He's really sorry, you know. It is possible to do bad things and be sorry for them. He'll bring roses. It will have a romantic ending. Did everyone here think you were a bad one too? Were you? If you were, I wouldn't mind. What did you do?

It is good to have a friend, Maurice. But some of the things my friend An tells me scare me. I think perhaps the air here, or the water, disagreed with her.

⟡   ⟡   ⟡

Anouk's diary, 29th March 1971. Liversall collection.

H is the hospital. H is the hospital.

My headaches have increased in the past few days – more of them and more painful. Yet somehow this thought struck me like a message from God – when I was sitting on the toilet just now I had to get out my notebook and write it down. *H is the hospital.* I think he is stealing blood and feeding it to the hospital itself.[12] I am aware

---

12   This is unprofessional of me. This interjection. The interjection I am about to make. Forgive me. This is, as I have established, an unusual type of case study. There is no pro-forma for how a document like this should be constructed. I have established – to all the doubters and naysayers and tabloid readers and, one hopes, to my former and potential colleagues, to *everyone* – that Bridget was in the grip of serious and undiagnosed mental illness. I have – for the sake of full disclosure – made clear that the circumstances in which I construct this ground breaking work are far from ideal and my own personal feelings towards this girl – well, they are present – as present as the vigorous stalk of ivy that taps taps taps against the window I sit and type beneath.

You'll have an idea of what a psychiatrist is supposed to do in a situation like this. To sit impassively with his patient while she spouts – for hours and hours on end – the most self-serving, sympathy seeking nonsense you've ever had the misfortune to hear. You'll imagine me, perhaps, sitting with my patient, nodding sympathetically as she airs her paranoid fantasies, embellishes her tales of woe, and concocts a sexually charged delusion with some disguised version of myself or a respected colleague at its sticky, unwholesome centre. Their brains are like apples that have been infested by worms: chewed through and rotting. And you sit, and you smile, and you nod, and you make notes now and again, the pencil scratching, the clock tick ticking. And you say – well, very little. You don't tell them to *get on with it* or *come off it* or confess that if you were their mother you'd have battered them with a walking stick too – you don't say any of this. You don't say your arse is itching or you need the toilet or you drifted off for a moment there,

this sounds quite insane but it makes perfect sense. He could be tipping it down the plug holes. Piping it into the heating system. I don't know his madness exactly. What would happen, I wonder, if a doctor became sick and there was no other doctor around to examine him and to treat him? What if all the doctors here are sick? What if...

But no. This headache, it is too bad.

---

thinking about whether the canteen is serving lamb or mutton today. You don't say any of that.

So forgive me – dear reader – this interjection. When for the first time in my professional career I can interrupt a patient and say exactly what I want to say. My friend Dr Parag Kapoor was a strict vegetarian and the mere thought of him gallivanting around the fells on the hunt for stray livestock on which to perform unholy and entirely unauthorised experiments, resulting in him dispatching sheep blood into the hospital itself is patently, manifestly, untrue. The building itself is in the process of being utterly ransacked. I believe they're unscrewing the heaters from the walls and capping off the old pipes as I type. Nothing spills onto the floor except water. Only water. I should have asked Parag if he'd ever turned her down. He'd have been too gentlemanly to tell me the truth, I expect. He was like that.

Plunge Hill: A Case Study

Item is a letter, handwritten on the back of a parish council notice. The notice outlines the dates of special services to celebrate the 80th, 90th and 95th birthdays of members of the parish. Liversall Collection.

Dear Maurice,

Tonight at Canasta Club Mrs Appleyard told me that there's a special well or a spring out in the grounds of the hospital, and that people collect the water from it in plastic bottles and feed it to their plants, because it's supposed to make them live longer. Someone should tell Miss Liversall about that – because no matter how much she preens and tends to those things, the lot of them are dead. That's the well An was writing about in her diary. Apparently, all of the natural springs in this part of Lancashire – the Trough of Bowland, it is called – have these little stories and myths attached to them – sprites and boggarts and the ghosts of children who played too close to the edge and drowned in them – their voices just about audible in the tinkling of the water, or in the echo of your own voice as you whisper your secrets down the well to be rid of them.

'You won't go looking for them now, will you love?' said Mrs Maywell.

'Of course not,' I said. And an image came to me – not of a spring or a well or a natural pond, but a lake – a big neat man-made boating lake – rather like the one in my dream, but all frozen over. 'Frozen lakes can be dangerous,' I said, not really knowing what I was talking about. 'Accidents can happen.'

'Yes,' Blackheath the second said, edging away from me as if I had threatened him. 'Yes. You could say that.'

'You just stick close to the hospital and you'll be alright love,' Mrs Appleyard said. She reached out to pat my shoulder, then drew her hand away – as if whatever sickness I had (I do think I might be a little unwell, Maurice – or at the very least, very overtired and not adjusting to the change of moving here) might be catching.

Water is just water, whether it comes from a well or a spring or an ordinary old kitchen tap. It's all the same. I won't listen to any more silly stories about it. But the Canasta Club, all brought up here and went to school here and never left – still half believe them.

Did Mum and Dad tell you about my boss, Dr Kapoor? About the work he's doing up here? I know – I do know – you're sick to the back teeth of hospitals. But – well – ask them about it. Ask them if you can all come up and visit me here. I'll show you where I work. You can meet him. I think he could help you.

Brix-and-Stones

ぞ ぞ ぞ

Anouk's diary, 30th March 1971. Liversall collection.

I fainted at the hospital yesterday. It is the afternoon – it is still light enough to write this without the candle. I slept all night and all morning. I am in the cold, small bed. Miss Liversall must have some human sympathy within her because she has brought me tea in a teapot and a slice of bread and real butter. I will eat it.

I fear I may be feverish. I find myself thinking I wish I could go home, not to Sweden, but to Newcastle: despite everything, I was happy there. Or, at least, I was happy to begin with, when I still had hope. And, lying here with nothing to occupy me but my thoughts, I remember that happiness and I know my mind exaggerates it, blots out how it ended, and yet I cannot help but bask in it – the busy city, at once rough and homespun, yet also outward-looking, welcoming. I stare at the cracks in the ceiling beyond the canopy and imagine I am once again drinking in The Jubilee, dancing in Luckies or watching bands in the Lorcano and the City Hall, all with Clive and his curly moustache. The locals disliked me, but I was happy because I had a dream which was fulfilled in Newcastle, a dream of England. Ah, I wish I had the money to go back.

But then I remember that money is not the issue. I can never go back to Newcastle. Those memories of happiness are a lie.

The final thing I remember from yesterday was that I was sitting, typing up Dr Kapoor's notes about H, when I heard the distant squeal of Blackheath's trolley wheels trundling along the corridor, heading towards the typing pool. Without much of a plan on where I would go, I stood up from my typewriter, determined that I would not sit there if the man was going to accost me and accuse me of being a criminal. I made it to the toilet, shut the door to my cubicle. I remember sitting down and I remember the floor swinging away from me quite suddenly, the walls lurching, and then I was on my side with one arm underneath me and blood coming from my eyebrow where I had hit it on the door's bolt lock as I fell. Hazily, I remember the loud crack of the door being forced, and

legs – all around me. Chapcott's bare white legs and the
stockinged legs of the other typists all around me like the
stalks of strange flowers. Amid the chatter I could still hear
the trolley wheels getting closer and in my head I could
once again feel Blackheath lunging at me on the village
green, could hear him spitting the word *Clive* at me.

Everything went black – not power cut black but
a milky black, just a shade away from grey. I saw the
chandelier from the ceiling at The Jubilee circling past
me just like a time when Clive and myself were there one
evening and he had rushed in to kiss me, with such passion
and such drunkenness that I had laughed, throwing my
head back, and he swept me across his knee, bending to
kiss me like the sailor in that famous photograph of the
end of World War Two. I think it must have been New
Year – midnight. His knee had dipped too low and of
course he lost his balance.

I crashed back into the room. Mrs Chapcott was
telling me to lie still, and in a hospital there is always
a doctor, and in the basement our nearest doctor is Dr
Kapoor so of course it was he that would come. Around
her I could see the typing girls. I had thought they would
be laughing at me, but they were not. They were simply
staring, scared. I began to search the faces around me,

expecting Blackheath to pop out at any second, leering and stooping and saying, 'Clive.'

The room set off again, like a roulette wheel. I caught a glimpse of the St Nicholas Cathedral, whisking past as Clive and I sat on an empty bus, on the upper deck. It was spring, very early in the morning, and we were returning home. He had asked to put his hand down my top and I had said no, but of course he had gradually done it anyway and here we were. I had stared out of the window, watching the city pass by, while he fondled away at myself and himself, and then I had closed my eyes. I heard the notes of the cathedral bells as they rang, cascading across the rooftops, the cars and the people, as Clive pulled down at my top, letting my breasts spill out. I was there and very far away at the same time. I felt the bus come to a stop and I had opened my eyes again to see another bus had pulled up next to ours, and I was now alongside a trio of boys, about ten or eleven years old, close enough that they could reach across and touch me were it not for the two windows that separated us, muffling their thuds and their whooping. I lifted my hands to cover myself but Clive, laughing, pinned them in my lap.

Clive melted. I found I was back in the cubicle, flailing at Dr Kapoor, my arms resisting him as he knelt to test my pulse. *Pop.* Something spiked inside me, as though a giant hand had seized and was shaking me. I spasmed. '*Inte du!* I hissed. 'Get off me! *Rör inte mig!* I could see that I was trying to lift a leg to kick Dr Kapoor away but his arm held it down. Images strobed into my head, like a nonsense zoetrope: a thicket of rhododendrons, a cracked block of concrete, a still surface of water, a vanishing hand at the pub window, the typists' trembling fringes, Clive's face disappearing, Kapoor's bloodied overalls – purloined blood. Was he part of this *we*? This group who somehow know about Clive? What did they want? I shouted, wordlessly, seeing my spittle arc in numerous directions.

I heard Kapoor say, 'Can we give her some space, please?' and I found I was being wrestled up onto the toilet seat by him. I went docile at his dexterity, already feeling a little better in the sitting position, shamed by my rage, all fierce emotion leaching away from me, normality resuming. 'Everyone, please. Back to work. Thank you.' The girls dispersed, exiting the room, all of them except for Chapcott. Dr Kapoor's hand was soft and warm as he touched it against my forehead, feeling for a temperature, and pulled my eyelids down, peering in at what he could see there. He took out his stethoscope and listened to my chest.

'She's utterly exhausted,' he said, then to me, kindly, 'aren't you my dear?'

'The others are working just as hard as she is,' Mrs Chapcott said, perhaps afraid that she was about to be blamed for my condition.

'Immaterial.'

'This sort of thing has never happened before.'

'Look at her. It's as plain as day.'

'You want to ask Miss Liversall what she's been feeding her. You know how she is.'

Dr Kapoor went on to say that he thought I was anaemic, low in red blood cells and would need assistance with additional iron in the diet. He laughed. 'Ask a blood doctor what's wrong with you and he'll tell you it's your blood.'

I smiled. Dr Kapoor is a nice man after all.

'Do you mean I should be eating meat?'

'Some sleep should be sufficient. I shall take you home to Miss Liversall and advise her on your diet. I want you to get bed rest this afternoon and plenty of it.'

So here I am, staring at the folds in the canopy and the cracks in the ceiling above it and thinking of Clive. Clive with the curly moustache and that afternoon when everything changed. I had thought that the past was the past. That what has been done could not be undone. I had thought the dead move on and that life was for the living. I find I am now not so sure.

That afternoon, I left Bourgones, the pub where I was working, and got the 22 bus. It was summer and the city had a beauty to it: the gulls winged across the wide river, women in headscarves browsed Paddy's market, children in shorts picked through the rubble of dilapidated houses, chasing one another, laughing. The streets grew quieter the further east we went. I got off at my stop and made my way to the high wooden hoardings. There were no signs of labour here – no-one was visible, no sounds could be heard. I made my way through the site entrance.

'Hello?' Within the hoardings was a landscape of mud sectioned off by large concrete sleepers and occasional stunted constructions of scaffolding. In the distance I could see a few heads moving back and forth, men working on a sunken section in the mud, one of the basements Clive and his mates had dug out. I made my way over to them. As I did so I saw that the heads belonged to men who were merely on a wide step which led down to the true basement, a further ten or so feet below, accessible by a ladder wedged into the dirt.

'Hello,' I called out. The faces on the ledge appraised me, seeming mildly shocked at my presence. They don't get many women coming down here, I thought. 'Is Clive here?'

Clive came scurrying up the ladder at the sound of my voice.

'Anouk!' He stood on the ledge, beaming up at me. 'You came!'

'I did.'

His eyes were so full of joy, wide and alive above his ridiculous little moustache.

Oh, God.

I should sleep.

ぞ   ぞ   ぞ

Letter, typed. Dated 12th November 1972. Envelope missing. Condition: fair. Shipley collection.

Dear Maurice,

It is very late and I'm still at work, all alone, typing with the candle. In the after-hours in this place Blackheath does the rounds with a trolley, offering those little brown bottles of local ale that Miss Liversall likes, coffee and plain sponge cake to those stragglers doing their bit of overtime for medicine.

I don't have to stay late. I don't get paid any extra if I do. But I am avoiding sleep. I had my dream again last night: the thing in the water gliding towards me. I saw – but didn't see, not with my eyes – that the thing had a long shape, and moved by flicking itself backwards and forwards under the water like a whip. Its rapid movement caused ripples to spread out across the surface. The ripples overlapped each other and spread out over the entire lake, causing waves to break at the shore – and I stared at them for a long time, waiting for the thing to reach me. Its movements were horrible in a way I can't describe. I waited, my feet cold and frozen on the icy shore. And then I woke up.

I think it's a worm. A worm that lives in the water. And if I sleep too long…

Perhaps Dr Kapoor really is a nice man – Anouk seemed to be warming to him – and perhaps I should speak to him about my dreams.[13] But for now, I will

---

13   You'd think the silly girl would have thought to go to a psychiatrist, rather than a hematologist. Why Chapcott didn't send all her new recruits to me for assessment and supervision – especially the important ones – as a matter of course is utterly beyond me. I suggested it to her, of course. Many times.

J.M. McVulpin

'I don't think that will be necessary,' she said haughtily. I'd popped down to the typing pool – asked, I think, if any of the girls wanted a quiet chat with me. After hours. Privacy of my office. That sort of thing. It was in the aftermath of Gloria – or perhaps Holly – I can't remember and they are all much of a muchness in the grand scheme of things – and my concern was that the typing girls might have become attached, and found the sudden absence of a colleague discomfiting.

'My girls know their business, McVulpin,' she said. She never calls me 'Doctor'. I notice that. She doesn't think I'm the real thing. 'They know where to put their focus. They're fine. Look at them,' she gestured around her, at the bowed heads and the pale white fingers typing at speed.

'They're all so young—' I said. She interrupted me. I only meant – I want to be clear about this – that the girls were inexperienced. They were professionally green. Many of them away from their homes and families for the first time, and only embarking on the long slow drift towards adulthood and full psychological and physical maturity. That as younger colleagues I considered myself a kind of mentor to them. Capable of offering direction. Guidance. Perhaps even solace. I glanced at the empty desk. It was a little tradition they had. A ritual, I suppose. Keeping the desk in question empty from Easter Parade to Winter Lights. A mark of respect, Chapcott said. She did have a softness to her heart, though she liked to keep it hidden. But as I said, she interrupted me.

'Young. Yes,' she said briskly. 'And perfectly safe in my care.' I did not like her implication. I turned away and left, hearing a chorus of giggles and sniggers. I had the most peculiar sensation then – that if I'd have turned around suddenly to face them, I'd have found them working as steadily as they had been before, their blank impassive faces bent over their typewriters, my presence entirely unnoticed, and the laughter coming not from them, but from the building itself. A mere fancy – a defence, I suppose, against an unpleasant professional humiliation. None of us are immune to the problem of being human, and I forgive myself entirely.

work. Patient H is unwell and remains unresponsive to treatment. She declines rapidly. Kapoor is worried. I will help him and ask him to help you before I ask him to help me. Good people – and I want, very much, to be a good person – are not selfish.

I typed that an hour ago. Just as I reached to load a new piece of paper into my typewriter, the lights went out. There was no warning, no announcement. I fumbled for the candle on the corner of my desk and found it, but I wasn't able to find my matches. I groped about for them for a few minutes then just decided to sit it out. So there I was, sitting in silence, in total darkness, waiting. I didn't like it. What if I fell asleep sitting upright here at my desk? What if I dreamed? The petrol generators will kick in any second, I thought,[14] but, if they were going to kick in,

---

14   Bridget is right here, of course – the generators should have taken over providing power from the hospital. What are we to read into this? Another one of her hallucinations? An error in thinking or writing – or an out and out untruth? In her defence, this may be neither. During the period that Bridget is writing about – when the whole country was held to ransom by the unions and crippled by irregular power cuts – there were several occasions when I, as she did, worked late at the hospital. When I, as she did, partook of the evening cake rounds, and when I, as she did, sat in the dark, waiting for the generators to kick in. It is hard to keep your wits about you at such moments.

they were certainly taking a while. So I stood and felt my way to one of the neighbouring desks and began touching around, trying to find my neighbour's book of matches. No dice. I moved on to the table in front but before I could start my search I heard a horrible noise coming from Dr Kapoor's rooms.

We're too far away from the wards and the theatres to hear whatever goes on there – thank goodness. So it couldn't have been that. Perhaps Dr Kapoor had fallen and hurt himself? I found the wall and guided myself along it, out into the corridor, towards his room. I had steeled myself and touched a hand to the knob when the lights quietly flickered back on. I heard two dull thuds, then silence. I was listening so intently that I literally shrieked when the corridor door behind me burst open and Mr Blackheath came through with a trolley for the incinerator. He usually stops to say

---

Hard not to scream down the maw of a darkened stairwell for Blackheath, whose work it is to maintain and fuel the generators, and who you are perfectly sure has just failed in his duties, leaving the less essential ventricles in the dark. Nothing more than that. But as the seconds stretch into minutes and the darkness continues – a darkness so thick that you can't even see your own hand in front of your face – and you grab blindly for the rail in the certain knowledge that if you lose your footing you will plunge down the stairs to a broken neck – or worse – it is hard not to let certain faulty ideas take hold. I do pity Bridget here. Many of us are afraid of the dark.

hello, but he was rushing along – his face dripping with sweat – and I don't think he even noticed me. In turn my shriek had caused Dr Kapoor to come out of his office.

'Did something alarm you, Miss Shipley?'

'It was just the power cut,' I said, feeling desperately stupid.

His eyes searched mine. 'Yes, well… all over now.'

'Yes, it's funny,' I said. 'They're not usually over so quick.'

'That's true,' he said, without much interest. Then, as if only now registering the time. 'Do you often work late?'

'Not often, no. But…'

He waited for me to finish, and I couldn't.

'I wanted to help,' I said, in the end. 'My brother. My brother's sick too. And…'

He placed a hand on my arm. 'Yes,' he said. 'The leukaemia. The accident. A very tragic case.'

The door to his office was slightly ajar again – all the candles inside lit and flickering and casting horrible shadows along the wall and ceiling. He sighed deeply, squeezed my arm gently, and let it go.

'You look very tired, my dear,' he said. 'Are you quite well?'

I felt like I wanted to cry then. The night before I'd woken up standing in the bathroom. I must have got up in my sleep and thought it was morning because the plug was in the bath and the cold tap was running full pelt: it sounded like a waterfall and was two inches away from the overflow. I knelt and plunged my hands into the freezing water and pulled out the plug, turned off the taps, and watched the water drain away. It gurgled and burped away down the pipes and I listened for the voices of the sprites, the boggarts and the drowned children but heard nothing but my own ragged breath and Miss Liversall, snoring in her bed. I was lucky I didn't wake her up: she'd have gone spare if I'd have flooded her bathroom. The sleeves of my nightdress were soaked but I didn't bother getting changed, just sat on the edge of my bed and waited for the morning to come. I thought about that then – the sleepwalking, the business with the bathwater – and considered telling Dr Kapoor about it. But something stopped me. I don't want him – him most of all – to think I am a 'bad one'. Does that sound terribly mad, Maurice?

I tucked my hair behind my ears and stood up straight. 'I don't think there's a problem with my work, is there?' I said.

He sighed deeply. 'Are you having your nightmares again, my dear?'

'I'm fine. I want to help. My brother—'

'You do know I can't help your brother, don't you? Somewhere in your heart?'

'You're not supposed to give up hope on people,' I said. I wiped my face. 'You're supposed to help them.'

He passed me a handkerchief.

'I always try to,' he said. 'And I do understand how difficult – how impossible, even – it is sometimes, to face the things that happen in spite of our own best intentions…'

'What is it? Is it the work? Is it not going well?'

He looked at me intently, as if hoping I would say something else. I should be like Anouk, Maurice, and speak less about personal things at work. It is not professional.

'No. It is not going well,' he said. 'Perhaps Mrs Chapcott was right all along, and we should have stuck to her traditional approach. The criminals, the drifters. The unwanted. Those who wouldn't be missed, who wouldn't be mourned by their families – but would find, perhaps, a bleak kind of peace in becoming a greater part of the workings of Plunge Hill,' he caught himself. 'But this – this doesn't concern you.'

'I could help!' I said – it just slipped out. Louder, and more passionately than I meant it to. Then I was ashamed. As if a typist could do anything that a doctor couldn't. He only smiled again.

'I do not think you really want to help me,' he said.

There was another soft thud from his office – or from the room next to it, perhaps. Books falling from a bookshelf? Or a large bird – perhaps an owl – accidentally colliding with the windowpane? He frowned, looked over his shoulder and turned back to me.

'I must attend to my work. Go home, Bridget. Ask Mr Blackheath to drive you. Go home to Miss Liversall and get some sleep. If you are disturbed in the night, come to me tomorrow and I will give you something to make the dreams you have about your brother go away.'

He withdrew into his office and closed the door behind him and I stood there out in the corridor for a moment longer, listening to the sounds of Mr Blackheath's trolley squeaking along the corridor on its return trip from the incinerator. Did Mum and Dad speak to you about Dr Kapoor? Are you going to come and visit?

The power went out again. I just had to stop and light the candle. It flickered just now: as if someone had tried to blow it out. As if the very air around me was vibrating. It does strange things to you, this place. Mum and Dad really hate me, don't they? They couldn't wait to get rid of me when the letter from Plunge Hill dropped through the post box.

Plunge Hill: A Case Study

Where is bloody Blackheath?!!!

I could go and sit at Chapcott's desk and use the phone that is sitting there. It's late. Mum will be in bed, hair wound up in her headscarf, her face all shiny with cold cream. Her slippers – the blue ones with the fluff across the top – lying neatly side by side at the bathroom door, in case she's up in the night. And Dad will be downstairs listening to his records. He'll have waited until he's certain she's nodded off, then got out his bottle of whiskey and poured himself a little tot of it. Maybe a cigar too, if it's been a hard day at work. I wonder if they still do that.

Everything got different after you got ill, Maurice. I'm not saying I'm blaming you – it wasn't your fault and nobody asks to get leukaemia, I do know that – but still. Before you were sick – before you were born – the three of us were really happy. I'd sit downstairs with Dad sometimes, listening to his records. He'd let me have milk out of one of the special cut-glass tumblers he liked to have his whiskey from while the music rose and swelled around us, Mum upstairs sleeping. Everything safe. Everything perfect. And then there was you.

I can't phone now. It would frighten Dad. Do you know how it aged them, every single time the phone rang and they thought it was a doctor with some results from your latest batch of tests, or some news of a blood transfusion that was supposed to help you, or a call back to hospital because your blood didn't look good? It got so bad that when Mum heard it ring she'd sometimes start crying.

'You answer it, Bridget,' she'd say, 'I just can't cope with one more thing. Not one more thing.'

If I rang now – in the middle of the night – I'd probably give one or the other of them a heart attack.

Sometimes my mind feels like his hospital – a great big stone building with solid walls, rainproof and windproof, standing strong and firm – and the hill is pushing against it, the soil and rock sliding forwards, inch by inch – and there's such pressure that one day there'll be a crack somewhere, and the whole thing will... I know Mum and Dad want you and not me, Maurice. I am struggling to remember – to know why that is. I think I do know – it is on the tip of my tongue – something to do with water, with ice – but as soon as I reach out for the memory, it evaporates. It is like trying to grab smoke.[15] Blackheath is here. Thank God!

---

15   The psyche always wants to be well – always wants to integrate the repressed, traumatic knowledge with the life story available to the conscious mind. Here, I would have applied two techniques.

Plunge Hill: A Case Study

❧   ❧   ❧

Anouk's diary, 5th April 1971. Liversall collection.

After a day spent resting, I am back at the hospital this morning.

Despite this rest I am tired. I was awoken early this

First, a light hypnosis achieved by asking Bridget to place her attention on some shiny object – most often a pocket watch, but a coin or the back of a teaspoon will do – while certain suggestions were made to her. Then I would have, very gently, coached her through the events of the day of Maurice's tragic accident – the ones that she could re-member – and through suggestion and urging – into the darkness to retrieve the detail that she could not access, but was there all the same, lodged in her subconscious and troubling it, as surely as a splinter in an eyeball would irritate and – eventually – go septic. If needed, I would have obtained and shared with Bridget various official documentations that are now in my possession for the purposes of collating this book. Newspaper clippings about the accident, the inquest, the circumstanc-es of her brother's death. The memory is one splinter – the splinter that infests and irritates, as you can see – but there is another one. And that is the desire. The motivation. A full return to health would have relied on Bridget fearlessly stepping into the darkness of her own mind and shining a light into its most frightening corners. Would she have been capable of it? Most of us are not, dear subscriber. Most of us, I believe, would rather live our entire lives on the surface, blissfully unaware of the violence that lies beneath.

morning by Miss Liversall coming into my room. She had made a clattering noise as she did so. I sat up and saw she was carrying a tray on which was what looked like beer, a half-pint glass filled with a dark, frothy liquid. As the sun caught the glass I saw it had an almost reddish colour.

'Didn't mean to wake you,' she said.

'That's alright.'

'Little drink for you,' she said, settling down the glass on the table beside my bed. I watched some spill over the side, splashing on the woodwork.

'Is this Plunge Porter?' I asked.

'Oh… why, yes,' she said.

'Beer? In the morning? Before work?'

'I didn't think you'd know what it was,' she said, a dim trace of something akin to panic in her voice. 'It's very mild.'

'It will do me good?' I said, sitting up.

'The world of good. It's made from our own local water, you see. Fresh from the well. We used to give it to children back in my day. It'll strengthen you.'

'I'm not so sure,' I said. 'Won't I be smelling of beer when I turn up to work?'

'Oh, they won't notice,' she said cheerily, and when I hesitated, 'It's Dr Kapoor's orders, I'm afraid. This or the tablets, he says. I'm sure he wouldn't give you anything unless he thought it'd make you better.'

'Very well,' I said. I picked up the glass and brought it to my lips. Beer for breakfast, I thought. These British. 'Bottoms up. Is that right?' A worry I had that it would be perhaps drugged and I would slip into a stupor was unfounded. Almost immediately I felt revived, as though I was awake for the first time in weeks. I could taste the minerals – the iron, perhaps, that is washed out of the hills by the rain and into the well. It was as if I was drinking the earth itself.

I placed the glass back beside the bed and gave Miss Liversall a grin. She smiled back – which was as strange as having the beer brought to me in bed was, she is not a friendly woman – but as I looked at her I saw something was wrong. She was wincing, a hand on the door handle to steady herself.

'Is everything alright, Miss Liversall?' I asked.

'Yes… yes.' she said. 'I suspect I just slept funny. I'd best leave you to it. You bring that with you when you come downstairs.' She gestured at the empty glass and I noticed that her fingers were curiously clubbed together. She shuffled out of the room.

I sat there, in my bed, feeling more and more human as the seconds passed, the dark liquid spreading through my blood, and thought about Miss Liversall. I kept replaying that cramped gesture she'd made with her hand, the way she'd shambled from the door to the side of the bed, spilling porter and making much more noise than usual. I realised that, for the first time, she had seemed an old woman. Previously, although she'd looked like one, there had been something in her demeanour, something, well, I'm not sure I'd call it youthful, but lithe and fluid – graceful for an ageing spinster. Perhaps she takes medication, I thought, for arthritis or some other condition which affects her muscles and co-ordination. Perhaps my drama the previous night had interrupted her medical regime.

With my affliction now alleviated somewhat, my head clearer, I wondered at my previous thoughts, about how everything seemed somehow connected: Clive, this strange town, a crumpled up photo, and Dr Kapoor's experiments. I had thought him a doctor who steals blood from the dead...? Had thought the hospital itself his patient...? Are such notions possible? I smirked at my previous self. Or, rather, I made an attempt to smirk at myself, at such absurd thoughts. Nonsense!

And yet – I raised myself from bed, dressed, and went down to the kitchen that morning – I found I could not set them down. Indeed, I clutch them to myself like a winning hand.

Some of the girls have drifted into the office. I watch as Kat, I think she calls herself, comes in. Her entrance is typical of the rest of them. She comes in slowly, shuffling, a hand to her head, wincing. She settles down at her desk, motionless, pinching the bridge of her nose and occasionally moaning. The sound of typing, muted and intermittent, fills the room.

Perhaps this is all some kind of obscure practical joke aimed at me. Or perhaps they are all hungover. Or perhaps, it occurs to me, they were all awoken as I was by what happened in the night.

Mrs Chapcott has come in just now. She too is looking tired and unwell. She entered, hung up her coat, picked up her clipboard and moved from desk to desk, exchanging a few quiet words with each of the girls. From time to time she patted them on the arm. When talking to one of the girls nearby I heard her say, 'Don't worry. It won't be long now.'

Eventually, she reached my desk. 'Anouk, I need you to get back to working on Dr Woodward's notes. They've been piling up all week and there'll be a new folder this afternoon.'

'I'm not to do Dr Kapoor's notes?' I said, quietly.

'That's right,' she didn't look up.

'Is everyone… alright?'

'Yes, they're fine,' she said dismissively, making notes on her clipboard.

'Are you sure?' I said. 'Everyone seems—'

Before I could finish my sentence a fat strand of blood had leaked from her nose and dripped onto my typewriter.

'Oh, good God… not now!' she said, turning away, the back of her hand to her face.

I stood to assist, a hand reaching for her shoulder, but she turned back to swat it away. 'Get your hand off me…'

❧   ❧   ❧

Letter, typed. Undated. Shipley collection.

Do you remember the time when we went ice-skating on the boating pond? God, nearly a year ago now, wasn't it? Just before Christmas. They had the lights up in town. You weren't as sick then, were you? Or were you having a good day? I don't remember. I was going out to skate, and you cried and cried and Mum and Dad said I should just go, and leave you to it – that you were too sick to go. But then they were – I don't know – somewhere else? Why can't I remember? There's a gap here, I guess. My memories of our lives together in London are like a leaf that a caterpillar has been munching on. And it is still munching. Things I knew I could remember yesterday or the day before aren't there today. It's the water here. Washing things away. I remember Mum saying, 'You just go on your own, Bridget. Don't be silly,' and I remember looking out of the window and imagining myself going to the park – on my own – and feeling sorry for myself, because I did everything on my own in those days. I see the dark lake – the one in my dreams – flicker through my thoughts, and my feet are wet, then all of a sudden in my mind's eye we're on our way to the park with our winter coats on. It wasn't far for you to walk – only a mile or so, but I had to carry you. I remember that. How light you were. You were only four years old. Too big for a pram. But small for your age. And you were laughing and I was laughing but looking over my shoulder too, knowing that I'd get an absolute rollicking if Mum or Dad saw I'd brought you out in the cold. I only wanted to give you a nice day. I remember how thick the ice was. Your nose was all red. I was so busy watching the ducks waddle across the surface of the ice – looking for a way in to the water, I suppose – that I forgot to[16]

But I should work. Kapoor's notes have arrived: they are, as he tells me, a matter of utmost urgency. Life and death, no matter what Chapcott says. I'm only a typist, but I'm a life-saver too.

Brix. X

ঽ   ঽ   ঽ

Anouk's diary, 11th April 1971. Liversall collection.

It is 4 o'clock in the morning. I awoke a few minutes ago and picked the photograph from under my pillow. I turned my bedside lamp on, reached for a pencil and gently shaded over the name on the reverse. I had seen this done in a Hitchcock movie Clive had taken me to see in Newcastle. In among the soft grey scribble were the unmarked indentations where the pen had pressed down,

---

16   On Bridget! What courage! Don't stop there, I urge you!

leaving the trace of a name, illegible but for the shape of the name I was expecting and did indeed find: Holly. I jumped at the sight of it, dropping the picture in-between the side of my bed and the bedside table. I jammed my hand down to try to retrieve it and, in doing so, pulled over my lamp. It hit the floor, flickering out.

I sat for a moment, listening to hear if the noise had awoken Miss Liversall. When it seemed as though it hadn't, I decided it was nonetheless a good idea to see if I could find a replacement bulb before she found out.

I left my room, slipped down the stairs and into the kitchen. I looked through the drawers where one would expect such things: under the sink, where the shoe polish and old screws are kept, in a cupboard by the back door where Miss Liversall keeps an umbrella and gloves. Finally, I spotted a metal tin on top of the pantry cupboard. I pulled a chair over, stood on it and pulled it down. When I opened it I sighed a relief: light bulbs, half a dozen or so of them wrapped in a piece of fabric. I took one out and was about to close the box when something stopped me. The piece of fabric, I saw, was patterned with irregular crimson brown shapes on stripes of pale yellow and cornflower blue. I removed the light bulbs, set them down on the floor alongside me and lifted the fabric up in front of me. It was unmistakeable. This was Holly's shirt, the one from her picture, badly soiled with dark patches which – I sniffed at it – gave off an unpleasant copper aroma. Blood. At the centre of each of these patches was a tear in the fabric.

My heart thumped in my chest, so hard it felt as though it was stoppering the air in my lungs.

Holly had been stabbed. Murdered. That much was now obvious. But – the creak of pipework somewhere above me caused me to replace all the items in the metal box as quickly as I could – what had Miss Liversall to do with it?

ϿϾ   ϿϾ   ϿϾ

Letter, handwritten, in envelope. Addressed to Maurice and postmarked 15th November 1972. Shipley collection.

Dear Maurice,

Let's not talk about sad things any more. *Enough of your nonsense, Bridget Jeanette Shipley!* as Mum would say.

Anouk thinks Patient H – Holly – is dead. That good old Miss Liversall did away with her. But I think Anouk was mistaken because I spoke to Dr Kapoor only a day or two ago and he is still spending all his time on treating her – trying to save her. I went on a bit of a treasure hunt today. To find Patient H. I want to help. I don't want to get diverted, as Anouk did. I'm not ready to give up, Maurice. Not on Kapoor, and not on you, either!

First along the corridor to the long, cool, dim rooms where we store the patient records. I snuck out while Mrs Chapcott was on the phone – barking orders at someone she's got looking for Anouk. Apparently she left something behind, or they need an address to send her last pay packet on to. Whenever she's not doing anything else, she's working through old phone books, ringing up landlords and employment agencies, giving her name and trying to find an address for her. I thought of An's diary, tucked inside my pillow back at Liversall's, and said nothing.

Anouk might have been misguided and paranoid but she wasn't stupid: if she wanted these people to know where she was, she would have told them. So I said nothing, but crept out and down towards the records rooms. All the patient records are supposed to be filed there nicely in alphabetical order in their little yellow packets, and most of them are, but now and again, as you walk along, there's a little landslide of them on the floor, or a box or two piled against a wall where some lazy administrator has got bored of her filing and just wandered off. People go down there to skive, you know. More than once I've disturbed a Blackheath lurking in a corner smoking a pipe, or leaning against a wall reading an old newspaper. I've even spotted Mrs Maywell down here before, lounging around on an old wheelchair eating chocolates and flicking through *Woman's Realm*.

Today though, luck was with me and it was quiet and I went straight to 'H'.

'Right, An my friend. Let's find out what was going on here, shall we?'

I didn't realise I'd spoken out loud and my own voice made me jump. I coughed – embarrassed even though I was quite alone – and got to work. It isn't rocket science. But there were three long shelves full of H files and after flicking through them for twenty minutes – *heart attack*, *uterine cancer*, *brain haemorrhage*, *emphysema* – and seeing nothing about a blood study, the futility of what I was doing, the stupidity of it, just washed over me.

Needle. Haystack. Brix, you bloody idiot!

But did I give up? I did not, Maurice. I thought of An, going a bit stir crazy over her little bottle of Plunge Porter, getting paranoid perhaps, in her loneliness, and decided I would persevere. It felt good, Maurice – to be busy. To be productive. It felt, in some strange way, like I'd been able to shift myself and do something to outrun whatever it is that comes for me under the water in my dreams. Does that make any sense? Probably not.

Kapoor made it sound like he was trying to save a life, so I trotted back up the stairs and went to the palliative care ward. That's where the goners are. The nurses know who I am now – they see me pushing my trolley of files around often enough – so they only nodded at me as I went through the double doors, past the station and through to the bay where the beds are.

It was horrible, Maurice. They were all yellow and pale. Some of them hooked up to machines. Tubes in noses, masks over faces. The smell, too. All that death. They weren't dead, but it was coming for them, Maurice. It was on the way. Flicking its tail as it sped towards them under the cold black water. And they knew it too. Knew the worm was coming. There was a radio playing, and a little black and white television on castors showing snooker at one end of the ward. Those who could sit up had their faces kind of propped towards it, but nobody was watching. Not really. They were waiting.

'Is there a Miss or Mrs H on the ward?' I called, very faintly. Nobody answered so I spoke up again. I had a file in my hand – I was going to make the excuse that I was checking something to do with the study, or wanted to update a consent form or get a signature. 'Mrs H? Is there a Mrs H here? I need to check—'

A hand on my wrist. Cold. Gripped on tight, like a bloody vice. Chapcott, of course. The Matron had caught sight of me, didn't like what she saw, and had called down. Foiled. And I never heard her coming – the woman seems to be able to walk without touching the floor.

'Miss Shipley? What are you doing up here, interfering with the patients?'

It was a question, but not a question, if you see what I mean.

'I wanted to check something…'

'Were you sent up here? Did I send you up here to a ward? To disturb the sick and,' she lowered her voice, 'dying, and to obstruct the nurses in their duties?'

'No, Mrs Chapcott.'

'Perhaps a doctor did? Perhaps one of the consultants

summoned you up here with express instructions to…' she took the file from me with her spare hand, never letting go of my wrist, 'to bring Mr Heartworthy's personal records of his… what's this? His varicose vein stripping, onto the ward? Is that what happened?'

'I'm helping Dr Kapoor,' I said.

Chapcott narrowed her eyes at me: hatred and hope, all mixed together. 'He sent you up here? He's made progress? He sent you up here? To test…?'

'Yes. To collect the test results. That is correct. And I believe he's the doctor around here, isn't he?'

She laughed.

'You stupid little…' she turned away from me. The nurse in charge had approached, but was hanging back slightly, as if fearful that we were about to come to blows and she would have to intervene in front of her patients.

'I'm so sorry about this, Matron,' Chapcott said, and tugged my wrist, pulling me back past the nurses' station, through the double doors and onto the corridor, all the while muttering to herself about the time – about the Winter Lights fast approaching, and no progress made, and no more time to be messing about in laboratories, and Maurice – I think she's quite, quite mad. Either that, or she was drunk – I could smell the porter from the cake trolley on her breath.

'Holly? Are you there, Holly?' I called – in desperation – and Chapcott only laughed and pulled at my arm.

'Holly's long gone, you silly little fool.'

We went back down to the lower ground floor in silence, and she pointed at my desk, my typewriter, and I sat down without speaking.

I could do it again, couldn't I? At night? Stay after hours and have a proper look, when the nurses are dozing in the dayroom and Chapcott has gone home? I could do that. I'll see what An says. But maybe I will. I'll find H, and ask her if she'll help get you better first. Would you like that, Maurice? To get better?

Bricks-In-The-Wall

❦   ❦   ❦

Anouk's diary, 11th April 1971. Liversall collection.

Devils. Witches. Lunatics. Ah, Anouk – what have you wandered into this time?

Against my better judgment I have come into work. I

am, mercifully, alone, the other girls having taken a break to pick flowers.

The irony is that last night I went to bed feeling better than I have felt for a long time. The day had been bright and pleasant, the town I found myself in pretty – even my absurd bedroom looked elegant in its light. I was in a small town with small-town ways, I thought. But it was a beautiful town nonetheless. Who could entertain morbid fantasies in such a place? I even felt perhaps I was on the first step towards settling in, towards being untethered from my past and becoming one of them, becoming English. My suspicions of this place seemed ridiculous. I was simply experiencing the guilt I believed I had made my peace with. That and my illness, anaemia having starved of blood the part of my brain which allows me to see the world properly, letting paranoid nonsense loose from the dark corners so they could take over.

Or so it seemed. Then I came downstairs in the night and found the bloody shirt.

I had spent the rest of the night awake, naturally. I had made a plan that, when the sun arose, I would leave. It would be difficult to escape the house without causing some noise: the door is heavy and opens and shuts with much creaking of the hinges and rattling of the letterbox, but perhaps such noises, I posited to myself, would blend in in the morning. And so I tiptoed down the stairs just after 6:00AM. I stopped at the front door, wondering whether I should go to the kitchen and retrieve the shirt once again, the unnatural contents of the metal box seeming at odds with this natural light streaming in through Miss Liversall's stained glass.

The questions tumbled over one another to present themselves. What is Dr Kapoor up to in all this? No, he is not Dr Kapoor. I do not know who he is, but he is no doctor. Who is the man with blood on his overalls? What are the notes I have been typing up if they are not his medical notes? Who are the women I spend my days alongside if not fellow typists? Devils, witches, lunatics, all of them. What is real and what is not? Has the whole thing been laid on for me? A performance for Anouk? What would I do? Where would I go?

'Is everything alright?'

I jumped at the sound of Miss Liversall's voice. I spun around to see her standing on the stairs in a long dress of white cotton.

'Oh,' I said. She was attending to her hair with a brush. 'You gave me quite a fright. You are… going to a wedding?'

'A wedding?' She frowned at me, puzzled, then looked down at her clothes. 'Oh… no, not a wedding. Today is Good Friday.'

'Ah,' I said.

'The first day of our Easter celebrations,' she said, seeing my confusion.

'Well… I'd best be getting to work.'

'Very well.'

I exited the house, sensing her at a window behind me, watching me as I moved. So I was to go to work. I had no grand escape plan beyond trying to act naturally.

Outside, the town was oppressive. The house across the road, the one next door, the one on the corner – are they all in on it? What is *it*? I walked to work quickly, looking around.

At the hospital the girls all arrived in long white dresses similar to Miss Liversall's but also they were wearing summer hats covered with flowers. Bonnets, I learned they are called. They all have pretty hairdos and makeup on. Perhaps strangest of all, they have been nice to me, all of them, asking me if I would like a cup of tea or if would like to use their lipstick, smiling at me rather than sneering.

Mrs Chapcott too made an entrance in a white dress. *Made an entrance* is precisely what she did, to theatrical *oohs* and *aahs* from the girls, not just at her immaculate dress, but also her perfect hair and her bonnet, more a wreath of hollyhocks and sky blue squills.

'I did not know how seriously everyone takes Easter here,' I told her when she came over to my desk later in the morning, smiling nervously. I was trying to make conversation. Despite the situation, I felt faintly embarrassed to be sat among such angelic women in my drab tweed skirt and unwashed blouse, a stray weed among the peonies in full bloom.

'Oh yes,' she said. 'The Easter celebrations here are... well, they're vital. The only thing which keeps us going,' she laughed. 'Easter Parade and Winter Lights. You must have something similar where you're from.'

'It doesn't really sound like my kind of thing.'

'Community is good for that. You give something, you get something back. Our Easter celebrations are simply marvellous. Oh, that reminds me,' she began to ferret about in her handbag, eventually pulling out a box of chocolates. She handed it to me. 'For you.'

'Oh, thank you.'

'An Easter gift.'

'Very nice,' I said. 'Well, I hope you have a good time later.'

'But of course you'll be there,' said Mrs Chapcott. It wasn't really a question.

'No… I'm afraid not,' I told her. 'I have to visit a friend.'

This caused – I wouldn't call it a silence in the room, but there was a sudden easing up in the typing, faces turning my way.

'A friend?' said Chapcott.

'Yes,' I said.

'Where are you meeting them? In Plunge Hill?' She primped at her hair, as though this information had left her dishevelled. 'Who are they?'

'Just an old friend,' I said. 'I'm going to get the train to Preston.'

'To Preston? When? After work?'

'That's right,' I said. 'Is that a problem?'

'No – no, no. Not a problem. But you must stop for a little while after work for our Easter celebrations though. Just for a little while. Fifteen minutes or so.'

'I'm really not sure.'

'But they'll be taking place right outside the hospital.' She gestured at the staircase. 'At the Plunge Hill well.'

'Oh, really?' I said, at a loss of how else to escape. 'Very well then.'

Her relief was visible.

The niceness lifted after that. Since then the girls haven't spoken. My leaving for this imaginary friend in Preston has cast a pall on the place. What is their plan?

So, I thought, I have a plan but also no plan. My plan is to get out, to get away from Plunge Hill and never to return. But how? I could just leave, I thought – just go to get some fresh air, and then keep going, through the streets, out through the trees, up over the hill until I reach somewhere else.

But then I tried it, snuck up the staircase and there they were, the old people of Plunge Hill: Miss Liversall, Mr Blackheath, the man who I'd seen singing the song about killing his wife in the pub, the little white-haired lady from the hospital shop, dozens of them, the men in their best suits and the women all in white or cream summer dresses, all picking flowers – handfuls of flowers, piles of them around the well.

'Anouk!' Miss Liversall shouted, waving at me. The faces of everyone turned towards me. I shrank back behind the door and descended the stairs again.

Letter, handwritten. Sent to Maurice at the usual London address, with the postmark dated 17th November 1972. Shipley collection.

Dear Maurice,

The worst thing has happened. The very worst thing. I am completely alone now. I am scribbling here in the dark. Can't even read my own writing. It's likely that the letters will all be jumbled and that you won't be able to read a word of this. You are not reading a word of this anyway though, are you? So it doesn't matter what the writing looks like. It's talking to you or the wall, I suppose. Or the well! Haha!

I settled in bed as usual tonight, but only read a little of An's diary, then the power cut out, so went to the airing cupboard to look for a candle. When I came back with one Liversall was in my room, looking very fiercely at me. She was leaning heavily on a metal and rubber crutch. I was going to ask her if it was her hip – if she'd fallen and hurt herself – she is so old that a tumble down the stairs would probably finish her off – but before I could speak she got started on me.

'I'm afraid we can't have that,' she said, gesturing towards the candle I was holding.

'I need to see, Miss Liversall,' I said, as mildly as I could.

'It's a fire risk,' she said. 'I don't want the whole place going up in smoke just because you've taken it into your head to…' She looked at An's diary, which was open on top of the lacy coverlet – and she came over and picked it up 'What's this?' she said, suspiciously, flicking through its pages.

'It's my diary,' I said.

'Yours?' she peered at it in the gloom, at Anouk's tidy handwriting, the even lines filled up with her thoughts and feelings and her impressions about the hospital, even her unflattering remarks about Liversall herself. It took all I had not to walk over to her and snatch it from her hands. She closed the book and fastened its little metal clasp and pursed her lips at me.[17]

---

17   Miss Liversall – whose name I have changed for the purposes of this case study – and who remains in excellent physical and mental health, despite her advancing years, was anxious for me to point out what should be clear to all readers. Just as Anouk's diary is a confection of fantasy and projection on the part of poor Bridget, written in the hours when she should have been contributing to the smooth running of the hospital (Mrs Chapcott affirms she had to warn the girl more than once about her dreaminess, her inability to 'stay on-task'), this scene too is entirely imagined. Bridget, perhaps assisted by some harmless hospital gossip and the mere presence of a few objects in her desk drawers – objects that have become totemic in their power to invigorate and complicate her fantasy life – has composed this scene for

'This isn't yours. How much of it have you read?'

She lurched towards me on her crutch. I stepped backwards – as if a tiny, frail old woman could really pose a threat. But she was furious.

'I don't... I didn't...' I stammered.

'How much?'

'Just a little. Just a page or two. She talks about the hospital. She had this room,' I felt my face flushing. The humiliation of it, Maurice. 'It feels like having a friend.'

She stared at me, shaking, as if deciding whether or not I was telling her the truth. The yellow light from the candle spread out around us, throwing her bent silhouette against the wall.

'The thing you need to understand is that the young woman who rented this room before you was a very silly girl indeed. A bad sort, with extremely fanciful notions about—'

'It's just something to keep me company at night. I've no friends here at all Miss Liversall.' I put my hand out. 'Please let me have it back?'

I could hear the sound of my own voice – pathetic and wavering. Exposed like that, in my nightdress and

---

her own purposes, and I remind my esteemed readers and subscribers to remember it should be treated entirely as a piece of fiction from a rapidly sickening mind.

bare feet. I have always had trouble with making friends, Maurice. Always. The girls in Brownies never invited me to their birthday parties. Later on, the hockey club crowd never invited me to go up Oxford Street shopping with them. I don't know why. Sometimes I am afraid that there's something wrong or bad about me – something that is very visible to everyone else, but isn't visible to me at all. Something that means they keep their distance, and I stay at home, alone. I've never known what other girls my age are really like inside. What they think about. What they do at the weekends, or how they spend their money. What they do with their boyfriends, even. Anouk's diary was a kind of window into all of that. I knew even as I stood there, shivering a little in the cold, that I would never be able to make Miss Liversall understand that. She won't remember being young. About how lonely it can be. And as soon as I realised that, I lost my temper, reached forward and tried to snatch the diary from her.

'Give that back to me. It isn't yours to take!' I said.

She stepped back quickly, clutching the book against her chest. She looked afraid. Afraid – of me!

'You stay back,' she grabbed her crutch and backed out, onto the landing. 'Stay right back.' I did as she said. She laughed bitterly. 'Oh ho ho. Now we get a glimpse of your true colours. Quiet as a mouse. All *yes please, Miss Liversall*, and *thanks for my boiled egg Miss Liversall*, but when push comes to shove we see what you're really made of, don't we?' The light in the landing fizzed and flickered into life, briefly illuminating her face, her hair tied up in a headscarf, her greenish skin shiny with cold cream. 'This is what I warned Ada about. No need to treat you like you're one of the bloody family. It only gives you ideas. Then you start...' she leaned over, coughed, banged her chest and started again. 'Ideas above your station. Liberties. You just...' she waved her hands in the air. 'Impossible. The whole scheme. Totally impossible! And this!' she shook the diary at me. 'Were you authorised to take documents home with you?' She didn't wait for me to answer, but took a breath and ploughed on with the rollicking, 'I didn't think so. Where did you get it?'

'I found it,' I said. 'I was just—'

'Don't say anything. I wouldn't believe a word of whatever nonsense you're straining to come up with anyway,' she said. She turned the book over and over in her hands.

'I was going to see if I could post it back to Anouk. She's back home now, isn't she? In Sweden? I could take it to the post office tonight.'

I held out my hand for the book and took a step towards her.

'There's an address in this book?' she looked at it, almost desperately, and I remembered Chapcott's frantic phone calls. 'An address in Newcastle? Or Sweden? Or somewhere else?' She opened the book and flicked through it, squinting and clearly unable to read much of what she saw. 'What did she write in here?'

'I haven't actually done anything, Miss Liversall. You've no reason to be this unhappy with me.'

She snapped the diary closed and blew all the air out of her nose, like a horse. 'I expect lies. I expect poor manners and abuse of the facilities. But this...'

'I've done nothing wrong!' I shouted.

She laughed. It was a cold laugh – almost cruel. 'Not done anything,' she muttered under her breath. 'This is the limit, Miss Shipley, and you have reached it. I have had enough of this. Absolute nonsense. This is Plunge Hill property and you have stolen it. I shall give it to Mrs Chapcott for safekeeping, and she will decide what to do with you.'

I was so angry I felt tears starting to come.

'I'll give it her myself,' I said weakly, and held out my hand.

'You'll do no such thing,' she said, blew out my candle and left, closing the door behind her.

Bitch. Bitch. Bitch. Bitch. Bitch. Bitch. She's taken An from me and you're the only person I have to talk to. I can still talk to you, Maurice? Can't I?

⸎   ⸎   ⸎

Letter, handwritten. Badly damaged, possibly tear-stained. Dated 21 November, 1972. Shipley Collection.

Dear Mum and Dad,

Please let me come home. I can't stop thinking about [illegible] ice and [illegible] creaking sound [illegible] shattered. I remember [illegible] and [illegible] on purpose.

Can you drive up and get me? I'll get another job [illegible] won't have to put up with me and [illegible] still your daughter even after [illegible] and Maurice [illegible] Could I take a [illegible] and cash at the post office? Not sure [illegible] would [illegible] and if you could just [illegible] worm coming for me.

J.M. McVulpin

ᎈ   ᎈ   ᎈ

Letter, handwritten. Dated 22nd November 1971. Liversall collection.

Oh Maurice, what am I going to do? Mrs Appleyard won't cash my cheque. She'll know about the diary from Liversall of course. My great and unforgivable crime. They've been waiting for me to make a mistake, all of them, and only pretending to be kind to me.

'What do you want with three hundred pounds?' she said. 'That's a bloody ridiculous amount of cash to have on you.'

I mentioned something about Christmas presents and new clothes. I'd sat up the night before and made a plan – something to do with the train station. A taxi, even. And in the morning, I'd forgotten what it was I'd wanted to do – only that I was supposed to go to the post office and see if I could get my cheque cashed. That little crack in my mind – my brain, or my memories, I suppose – is getting wider. I peer into it some nights, and see – what do I see? Rushing water and black, broken ice. That's all.

'You can't go walking around with three hundred pounds in your purse,' Mrs Appleyard said. 'You'd be mugged and raped and murdered and who knows what else!' she laughed, but then the laugh turned into a cough and she had to sit down. There was blood on the handkerchief she took away from her mouth, but she only folded it up carefully and placed it up her sleeve.

'Please. It's really important. You could just give me half of it. Even just fifty pounds. That would be enough.'

She shook her head firmly. 'I just couldn't. Not on my conscience,' she said. 'Now don't cry. Come on Bridget. There's no need. Will you drink some porter with me?'

I shook my head and turned away. I let the door jangle shut and walked very slowly back to Liversall's. She was watering the still-dead plants in her window and staring at me with a look of smug self-satisfaction on her face. She didn't say anything – she'll be waiting for Chapcott to do her dirty work for her, I suppose.

Wheat-a-Brix

⚘   ⚘   ⚘

J.M. McVulpin

Letter, handwritten. Sent to Maurice at the London address, postmarked 23rd November 1971. Shipley Collection.

Dear Maurice,

The strangest day at work today. I was dreading it – truly dreading it. It was still dark when I waited at the bus stop in the morning. I stood there, stamping my feet with the cold, my skin itching with the sensation that every eye on the village was on me. *It's just a diary*, I wanted to shout. Curtain twitchers. As if I'd committed some truly unforgivable crime and they were watching me trudge my way to the gallows, completely alone. I ran into Blackheath in the lobby, standing there with his mop and bucket. I lingered, not wanting to go in and face Chapcott.

'Morning, Miss,' he said gruffly.

'Blackheath. Can you help me? I need to cash a cheque. Mrs Appleyard can't do it. She says it's too much. Is there a bank? Can you drive me?'

He paused thoughtfully, leaning on his mop handle.

'Are you all right, Miss Shipley?' he said.

'I'm quite all right, thank you,' I said. I smiled, but there was no feeling in it – my mouth was dry, my lips sticking to my teeth. I am sure he could tell. 'I just need some money.'

He sighed deeply.

'It'll be easier on you, you know, if you just relaxed a bit. Just tried to go with the flow of things,' Blackheath said. 'We all have our place. We all have jobs to do. Do you think,' he said quietly, motioning towards the pink suds in his mop bucket, 'that I'm leaping for joy every single time Kapoor calls me in to clean up that butcher's shop of a den he calls his theatre?'

He reached out, as if to pat my arm, but drew back at the last minute. 'Just try to—' he said, gently, but he was interrupted.

'Blackheath! Are you bothering my girls again?' Chapcott called. She clicked over to us in her high heels. 'I've told you, over and over again, not to disturb my girls. Go on now, off with you! Bridget, you can come with me. I need a word.'

'Apologies, Mrs Chapcott,' Blackheath muttered, and scuttled away without looking at me.

Mr Blackheath's mop bucket is on wheels, and he holds onto the handle of the mop and pushes it in front of him. The wheels make the most horrible sound – somewhere between a scrape and a screech – and any time the castors meet an irregularity in the floor's surface, dirty water slops over the sides of the bucket. That's how you can tell where he's been. Some days I've been able to track him through the hospital, following the little drips and puddles of pink suds and stained water. The sound of the scrape, of the screech – it is like the creaking that ice makes just before it breaks. My mind keeps getting away from me. It's like there's been an earthquake in my head, and my brain is full of cracks and sinkholes I keep falling into.[18]

Where was I? Oh yes. My strange day. I was expecting her to tear into me right away, but she only watched him leave, then turned to me calmly. 'I think you know what this is about,' she said. 'Come.'

I followed her, not to the typing pool, but through a small door at the back of the room – her office. She likes to be out front with the rest of us, better to *supervise our*

---

18   Perhaps Jung would have been able to help Bridget out. His remarks on the psyche come to mind here, and if she had ever thought to consult with me about her developing illness, I would have shared them with her. 'Instead of being at the mercy of wild beasts, earthquakes, landslides, and inundations, modern man is battered by the elemental forces of his own psyche. This is the World Power that vastly exceeds all other powers on earth. The Age of Enlightenment, which stripped nature and human institutions of gods, overlooked the God of Terror who dwells in the human soul.'

antics, she says, so this is a room I have never been into. It's tiny, windowless and sterile. No personal photographs, no plants or knick-knacks. She removed her coat, sat down and opened her drawer. Produced Anouk's diary, which she carefully placed on her desk.

'This is a very serious matter, Bridget. Very serious. What do you say for yourself?'

'Nothing.' There was no point in trying to explain.

'This document. I am troubled by it. Very troubled. It is clear that Anouk was a very disturbed young woman. Don't you think?'

I said nothing. Anouk was my friend, Maurice. I know it sounds doo-lally, but there it is. She was my *friend*!

'And you will understand, having read the lot, I suppose,' she didn't wait for an answer, 'that there were very good reasons why we couldn't have her here anymore. No skulduggery or dark designs. Just a case of her being entirely unsuitable for the task at hand. She was not,' she said thoughtfully, lifting open the diary with a fingernail and letting it fall closed again, 'a very sensible girl. Now was she?'

'I don't know what you're talking about,' I said, wondering all the while what was in the rest of the book – the parts that I hadn't yet read, and being determined as I could to get it back.

The next thing Mrs Chapcott did was very strange indeed, Maurice. I'm sitting here at my desk pretending to work on Dr Woodward's notes, but trying to sort it all out in my mind, and I just can't figure it out. *She smiled at me.* A warm, pleasant smile. Her face changed entirely and I realised, in a way I hadn't before, that in her prime she would have been a very beautiful woman. It was her work, perhaps, and the environment of this place, that didn't bring out the best in her.

'Now I'm prepared to overlook this, my dear. Provided, that is, that you go back out there and get on with your work. Try to forget all of this nonsense. It'll be the Winter Lights soon and we want to concentrate on that. On having a nice time together. It'll really make you feel part of things, and once you feel part of things, you'll be much happier. Can we call this a fresh start?'

'Can I have it back?' I said. Her smile vanished.

'Of course you can't, you silly girl. It's private property. Could even be of interest to the police, don't you think?'

The police? I bit my lip.

'Can I get on with my work, Mrs Chapcott?' I said. 'I don't want to get behind. Not with the Winter Lights coming up.'

She smiled again and the sunniness returned to her face, though not her eyes. 'That's the spirit, Bridget,' she said. 'Very good. Off you go.'

But before I'd settled into my seat, Dr Kapoor bustled into the room, right past all us typists at our desks, and met Chapcott at the door of her office.

'I have heard from Miss Liversall that there's been an incident,' he said.

'All dealt with. The mess has been cleared up. No thanks to you, of course,' Mrs Chapcott replied. He bristled and they went into her office and closed the door. The rest of the typists bowed their heads to their typewriters, all of us pretending not to listen to the fragments of what was clearly a heated argument filtering through the door.

'You've got to give up on this,' Chapcott shouted. Kapoor must have said something in return – I didn't hear – because the noise of her laughing bitterly floated through the walls. 'We've tried. We've all tried!' Her voice softened. 'You've done your best.'

He shouted back then. 'We don't know it will be the way it was in 1827! Nobody knows that for sure!'

'Go and ask Blackheath. He saw it with his own eyes. Ask him if he wants to risk it!'

I turned around in my seat. The girl sitting beside me – Kat, I think – separated by the empty desk alongside mine, was dabbing at her nose with a paper tissue. Our eyes met.

'What's going on?' I whispered.

'It's you, you idiot,' she whispered back, her voice hoarse. 'He's been trying to save your life. And now he's giving up.'

'Don't be silly,' I said. 'I'm not poorly. I'm just tired.'

Kat put her handkerchief over her mouth and coughed. The tissue turned red. She screwed it up and threw it on the floor with distaste.

'You're not sick. We are.'

Chapcott's office door opened. Kapoor emerged, his head down, his face flushed dark. 'You know what you've got coming?' Kat said, and coughed again. I tried to catch Kapoor's eye but he turned his head and walked past me as if I no longer existed.

'What?' I asked.

Kat hissed, 'You're for the worm!'

❧   ❧   ❧

Plunge Hill: A Case Study

Letter, typed. Unsigned. Dated 2nd December 1971. Shipley collection.

Dear Maurice,

The drab birds have started being nice to me. Drabber than ever, they've taken to dropping little presents into my in-tray. Lipsticks, half-used. Bars of chocolate. Little packets of salted peanuts. They stare at me. I feel like the picture at the back of the church we used to go in and light candles in front of when someone was sick.

Had lunch in the hospital canteen today. Mrs Maywell was there. I hardly recognised her. She'd aged since I last saw her. It was only a couple of weeks ago, I know that, but she was so stooped and pale she was having trouble lifting the ladle from the pan to my plate.

'Are you having my stew today, my lovely?' she said, as friendly and smiley as always. 'It's mutton. Mutton stew. All the doctors love it. You need a layer of fat on you in weather like this.' I like her accent. I could hardly understand it when I first came here, you know. But I've got used to it now. 'Are you finding it cold? Is it warmer, down south? Do you get warmer winters?' she was babbling, her eyes unfocussed, and I wasn't planning to answer her when she held my hand across the counter and said, 'You won't leave us now, lovely, will you? You won't go and run away on us, will you?' and I squeezed her hand and said, 'Where would I go, Mrs Maywell?' which seemed to satisfy her, and made me feel like bawling right then and there in the canteen.

I did hate you sometimes Maurice. I know it wasn't your fault but it wasn't mine either and I did. I did. When an injured animal screams and yowls and there's no way of helping you want to put it out of its misery and sometimes you want to put yourself out of your own misery too. Ignore me. I'm in an odd mood today.

Brix

❧   ❧   ❧

Letter, handwritten. Date illegible. Liversall collection.

Dear Maurice,

I went to see Dr Kapoor today. Just trotted along there with no invitation and rapped on his door.

'Ah,' he said, looking up from his papers. He gestured towards the chair on the other side of his desk. 'Do sit down, Miss Shipley.'

I nodded, and sat down. The office was a god-awful state: his white coat hanging from the top of an old standard lamp, and the anatomy posters on the wall peeling away from their fastenings.

'I want to know what happened to Anouk,' I said.

He opened a drawer and pulled out her diary: the thick leather-bound book, the little golden clasp. I'd recognise it anywhere – he must have got it off Chapcott during the argument.

'Of course you do,' he said. 'I can presume by the fact that you're still here, at Plunge Hill – that you haven't gone stark raving mad and run off into the hills – that you haven't actually read the entirety of her account, have you?'

'I was trying to make it last,' I said, wondering how I would explain.

'Yes. For the company,' he said, and nodded. 'At night.'

'That's it.' Miss Liversall must have told him. They all must talk to each other. About me. All the time. Does that sound mad? It does, doesn't it?

The diary lay on the desk between us. I could snatch

it up and grab it – and run away somewhere – lock myself into the ladies, perhaps, and read whatever it was that had got them all into such a tizz. The thought crossed my mind. And Dr Kapoor's too, I think, because he drew it towards himself slightly and looked at me carefully.

'Bridget. I ask this very seriously and would like you to consider your answer carefully. Have you considered that you might not really want to know the rest of Anouk's story? Her last days here at the hospital? Indeed, her last days in Newcastle?'[19]

---

19   I mentioned the nanny I had as a boy: her severity. I am reminded of her again now, reading here Bridget's little stories about the back and forth of Anouk's diary – a document that exists – it lies on my desk right now, along with the other papers and postcards from her suitcase – but which she obviously wrote herself. Truth is a funny thing, isn't it? Sometimes the very best way to hide a misdeed – I learned this at the hands of my nanny, schooled in deception by her severity – is to place it out in plain sight. Publish it widely for the entire world to see. When my nanny found the biscuit tin empty and called me before her, to stand, quaking in my short trousers, knees knocking before the voluminous expanse of her mega-bosom housed within the starched confines of that spotless white apron (the apron is the clearest abiding memory I have of her: the snowy front of it, and her hair, short and grey and trimmed close against the back of her neck – both snapshots tell me that I never dared to look her in the face) and asked me, very quietly, where all the biscuits were, I did the simplest thing I could have done. The wisest thing too, though I did not know it. I told the truth. 'I fed them to the dog, you nasty old cunt,' I said.

I answered immediately. 'I want to know what happened to her. And to Holly. And Gloria. And...' I don't know what made me say this. 'And the other ones. There were others, weren't there?'

Dr Kapoor stood up and reached for his overcoat. 'Very well. But you are going to have to be very brave, Bridget Shipley. And so am I.' He handed me the diary. I felt it, cool and solid and real between my hands, and felt very frightened. 'Come out and have a walk with me. Let's have some fresh air while the light lasts, and we will talk.'

Out in the grounds – circling the paved paths between the dead grass and empty flowerbeds – Dr Kapoor asked me if I knew about the Hippocratic Oath.

'We make this oath as young men and women, full of blind optimism,' he said, almost sadly. He walked slowly, his hands deep in his pockets, mine clasped around the

---

She looked at me, too shocked even to blink, and turned away. The matter was never mentioned again: I was not beaten. It's a lesson I've always carried with me. Something I told Kapoor, some time ago. In the face of gossip, of accusation, of blackmail, just – very simply – tell the truth. Shout it from the rooftops. Nobody will believe you and then you'll be safe. It almost always works. From that day forward Nanny never used her ruler on me again.

diary. I watched our feet: mine in my neat work shoes, his scuffed brown brogues trudging along the moss-spotted path. 'As soon as we begin, we find that it is almost never as easy as that.'

'You're supposed to make people better.'

'Yes,' he said simply. 'That is correct. But who is to say that – for example – putting chemicals into the bloodstream of a young boy that make him vomit and cause his entire body to cramp and ache and, in the end, give him mouth ulcers and cause all his hair to fall out – who is to say that that too, is not causing harm? Who is to say that, when very often surgery can look like butchery and what is intended as healing can feel – patients tell me this – very much like assault? Even torture.'

He spoke quietly and of course I thought of you, Maurice. Of all the things the doctors did to you.

'All doctors face this. Often very early in their career. The old person who has fallen and broken a hip, who might be eased into their final sleep with a dose of morphine that would also calm their fears and alleviate their pain. Does that do harm? Or does sending them to the operating theatre to be sawn and bolted and cut and stitched – an attempt to buy their joints a period of time that the rest of their body will not grant them – constitute the greater harm?'

'I'm asking about Anouk. Not a lecture in medical ethics,' I said. He chuckled softly.

'Of course. And I am getting to my point. But indulge me. Say a physician has a decision between two hurts – a minor one or a major one – well then, the decision is easy to make. Harder still, but not impossible, if the decision is between lots of minor hurts, and one major one. Harder still – perhaps even impossible – if the decision is between a mortal hurt – a death, is what I am saying – and the life – the life and health, of many many many others.'

'You're not making any sense,' I said.

'Then I will put it more simply,' he replied. Still we walked, not looking at each other. 'I am a very very bad man, Bridget. I have done the best that I could, and the thing that I have done is the most terrible thing.'

'To Anouk?'

'To you.'

I paused, suddenly feeling quite sick.

'I thought I could… an alternative plan. That plan has now failed. All my work has come to nothing. I see now that I have been very foolish. Foolish and unkind. And now I am faced with a most terrible choice, and the two of us – you much more so than me – are going to have to be very brave indeed.'

We waited on the path together. I stroked the cover of the diary, wanting to be away from there so I could read it. I didn't dare ask him what he meant. We carried on walking. It was cold – damp, as usual. The mist was gathering as we reached the edge of the grounds, where what used to be well-kept lawn met a little fence, and beyond that, dark hills and moorland. We stood at the fence for a moment and he watched me looking at the hills, at the darkness gathering.

'Do you see the well?' he said, and pointed it out. A small ring of old stones no larger than a car's wheel. Anouk's well.

'Mr Blackheath said there used to be a spring here. Magical healing water.'

He must have caught the mocking tone in my voice, because he turned to me and frowned.

'Don't be too quick to dismiss these old stories, Miss Shipley,' he said. 'That would be foolish. It might even be dangerous.'

'Is that what Anouk did? Dismiss your old stories?' I said.

We were totally alone and I should have been – it would have been wiser to be – more restrained, I suppose. But I was furious, and frustrated with his riddles. If he'd

have tried to do something to me – hit me or grab me or
even stuff me down that silly well[20] – there would have been

---

20   I do miss Dr Kapoor. We were… not exactly friends, but
close colleagues. We had, I think, a professional understanding. He
was – unlike some of my other colleagues who seemed to treat me
more like a filing cabinet or a light fitting or some other piece of
necessary but outdated furniture – respectful of my longstanding
position here at Plunge Hill. My experience with the building and
its history. My special relationship with the intricacies of hospital
culture. I remember the last time I saw him, when he came up to my
rooms bearing a bottle of Plunge Hill porter – for old times' sake.
He'd seen the way the wind was blowing and had come to tell me it
was time for him move on from Plunge Hill: a new position at a clinic
on the coast was calling to him.
    'No-one blames you for Bridget,' I said. 'You could stay.' He waved
his hand and shook his head: his decision had been made. 'When I
publish the case study,' I motioned towards my papers, or rather, Bridget's papers – I was just beginning to sort and order them at this point
– 'they'll see how sick she was. All this Home Office stuff will die down.
Chapcott will bring in a new—'
    'I'm sure you're right, Jack,' he said, clapping me across the shoul-
ders. 'You're doing a marvelous job. I see your light on up here almost
every night. Doesn't it bother you, being up here on your own?'
    'Where else would I go?' I said. I perhaps sounded more melancholy
then I felt, because he drew his chair a little closer to mine, sighed
again, and looked at me carefully. 'You are sleeping, aren't you – my
friend? Do you want me to prescribe you something…?'
    'I don't need sleep. None of us do. The work – the work of the hos-
pital is so very invigorating!'
    I laughed but he did not join in.

nothing I could have done about it. I wanted to shout then
– not because I was really scared, but because I wanted to
see if anyone would come: if my voice would carry all the
way back to the hospital, now only a dark shape in the mist
behind us – but somehow I knew it wouldn't.

'There used to be many sheep on these hills,' he said
softly. 'And I have used them, and they did not come back.
I was Anouk's friend.'

I looked away from the empty hills towards his face
then, thinking about the sheep and what he meant. *Used
them?* He did not break my gaze.

'It was Chapcott who wrote to you and asked you to
come here, was it not? You and Anouk both?'

'Yes,' I said, still staring, still wondering about the sheep.

'And you have not thought to wonder what that
means? What a young woman like you and one like

'This isn't the only hospital there is, you know. You can find somewhere else. Where were you before?'

I shook my head.

'You know, it's as if I was always here,' I said slowly. 'I remember
being a child. My nanny. Little scenes from school. That kind of thing.
And then,' I shrugged, 'here. Always here.'

'The world is a big place…' he said.

'Not for me.' I lifted the bottle of porter and drank deep. I have been
relying on it rather too heavily of late, I suppose. 'Plunge Hill is my home.'

Kapoor stood, squeezed my shoulder and left.

Anouk might have in common? About why Chapcott would want you for the hospital?'

It was almost entirely dark now. He reached forward and tapped the diary that I was still holding. 'Read it. You'll find out. And in the meantime... can you trust me? Can you understand that? I am acting for others as you, perhaps, believed you were acting for Maurice?'

'How do you...?'

I felt frightened then, and without waiting to see if Kapoor was following me or not, clutched the diary and ran away, back to my typing. At least I've got An back now. I'm going to get back to Liversall and read the rest of it and find out what was really going on.

❧   ❧   ❧

Letter, handwritten. Dated February 12th 1972

Dear Dr McVulpin,

Please find enclosed the letters and cards that you asked for. I trust these items will assist you in your investigation into the state of our daughter's mind in the weeks before her suicide. I hope you will understand that this has been an extremely difficult period for Mrs Shipley and myself and that we simply cannot make ourselves available for interview with you, nor are we able to correspond any further with you on this matter. We do not require the return of these items, and while we hope, as you suggest, that a study can be made that can help others and so bring some good from Bridget's short and misguided life, we do not feel the need to be informed further of your progress on this study.

In answer to your questions, please accept the following.

Bridget was, as far as we were able to tell, a very ordinary child. Quiet, perhaps a little dreamy at times, and not the most popular girl in the class but she tried hard at school and seemed to be well liked by her teachers. You will understand that her younger brother was quite seriously sick and he took most of Mrs Shipley's time and attention. During this time Bridget never made a fuss and was happy to help her mother around the house, etcetera.

No previous history of mental infirmity or alcoholism on either side that we know of. Both sets of grandparents enjoying a healthy and active old age, and all declining to be contacted further on the matter of childhood memories, medical history, opinions on recent events and similar.

Plunge Hill: A Case Study

The inquest at the time pronounced Maurice's cause of death as misadventure. You will be able to turn up these records yourself without much trouble, I suppose. We've seen Bridget's writings on the matter and we do know what we believe. This is something you will understand Mrs Shipley in particular finds nearly impossible to discuss and we would ask you to draw your own conclusions on the matter of culpability and its relevance to subsequent beliefs and actions, etcetera, on our daughter's part.

You'll have seen the stories going around in the tabloid rags: holes in the ground, black magic, earthquakes in strange places, orgies in operating theatres and so on. We've had journalists at the door before now and have had to change our telephone number again at not insignificant personal expense. We find this to be both an insult to Bridget's memory and a gross trivialisation of her inner troubles and the wider unease of our family. No, Bridget did not seem a particularly fanciful girl in her teenage years – we didn't allow horror films or that type of novel in the house so we don't know where she got this from.

Yours sincerely,
Mr M. Shipley

❦   ❦   ❦

J.M. McVulpin

Anouk's diary, entry dated as previously.

Once again I am in the toilet cubicle, after a morning of sitting, typing up notes and trying to pretend nothing out of the ordinary is happening. I needed a break from it all, so I have come here and brought you, diary, to try to piece it all together.

How am I to get out? Of this building, of this town? Escape has been the theme of life: from Uppsala, from Clive, and now from Plunge Hill. Or attempted escape, because clearly Clive has found me, in one sense or another.

Here is how it happened. I'd left Bourgones. I'd got my bus. I had thought the world beautiful, and now was looking down at him, at Clive, who was stood on the ledge below, grinning up at me, and he said, 'You came!'

'I did,' I said.

'Come down here. This way.' He had already started down the ladder.

'Down there?' I said.

'Aye, aye,' he said. 'Lads, she's here! Anouk's here!' He dropped down onto the floor below which I saw was not dirt at all but a surface of concrete. Around Clive men were assembling, setting down their tools, wiping their hands, removing helmets. I felt awkward, like a dignitary standing up high to regard them.

'One moment,' I said. I descended the ladder slowly, one hand trying to keep my skirt from billowing out. When I reached the bottom, Clive stumbled towards me and threw an arm round my shoulder. It stank down here, a fug of beer, cigarettes and urine. Rheumy eyes regarded me, looking me up and down, hands clenching and unclenching. Something began to knot up inside of me.

'Lads, this is my Anouk,' he said. 'She's *Swedish*. Go on, say something love, something in Swedish.'

'I don't know what to say,' I told them, attempting a smile. A few of them exchanged glances with one another at the sound of my voice – at the sound of my accent.

'Say that,' said Clive. 'Say *I don't know what to say* in Swedish.'

'*Jag vet inte vad jag ska saga*,' I said. There was a murmur in response to that – gruff, flatly impressed.

'I was talking to the lads about the troubles we've been having, y'know, with money. And they were thinking they could help us out.'

'Oh yes?' I said. I looked from face to face, finding nothing but inscrutable blankness, one man nodding, another chewing his lip.

'Yeah…' Clive stared at me, his eyebrows raised, as though waiting for a response from me.

'I'm not sure I understand,' I said.

Laughter from Clive. 'I think you do,' he said. 'Just think about it.'

That's when the penny dropped.

'No,' I said. I tried to step back, but Clive's arm tightened around my neck.

'Just think about it,' he said. 'Nearly fifty quid I've got you. It'll just take a couple of hours. And we've got a bed and everything.'

'A… a bed?' I said, incredulous.

The circle of those assembled parted and I was able to see a trench cut into the cement in which they had laid the cushions they'd stripped from an old sofa. Everything fell into place.

'I'm sorry,' I said, laughing, still casting about at the faces. 'There's been a terrible mistake. I shall be going home.'

'Come on, sweetheart,' said Clive.

'Get off me!' The rage had welled up inside me. I shook off his arm, glaring at him. What could I say? I wanted simply to not be here. No delicacy nor diplomacy could uncouple me from this ring of unclean, hungry men glaring at me from beneath their brows, treading slowly from one foot to another. How, I wondered, could I extract myself from this situation?

Clive laughed. 'Told you she was feisty,' he said, to some laughter. Then he leaned in close, a hand at the back of my head, stroking. 'Come on, Anouk. I don't want this any more than you do, I promise. But fifty quid, or near enough. Think about it. Just a one off, to help us out a bit.'

'I'm not doing it,' I said. 'I can't believe you've even come this far. The…the shame of it, Clive.'

'You could do them all at the same time, if you wanted to. Get it out of the way quicker.'

'I'm going home.' Was I going home? How does one go from a situation such as this to simply *going home?*

'Anouk,' he said, an edge to his voice, but he couldn't deliver on it, not with other men watching him. Or perhaps he didn't want to damage his goods. He lifted a pair of placating hands my way. 'Let's talk about this. Just talk. You and me.'

I said nothing, simply shook my head. I could feel the pull of conciliation at work in me. Anything to shut off the conflict.

'Lads,' Clive said. 'Listen, we're just going to talk it over in the pit.' He started to walk away. Naturally, I followed.

The pit, it turned out, was the foundations of another block identical to the one where Clive and his friends had made me a bed. We walked over to it in silence. There was a petrol cement mixer churning in the corner. The noise increased as we got nearer.

Clive dropped onto its mud ledge step and then descended its ladder. I followed, grateful to be out of sight of the other workers.

'I cannot believe you,' I said. 'What were you thinking? I almost think this is a joke. I'm not—'

As I reached the bottom rung I felt his hand at the back of my hair again, this time twisting, winding the hair into his fist. He yanked it back, hauling me onto the concrete. I managed to pull myself onto my knees. Clive crouched behind me, his arm now around my throat.

'It's going to happen,' he said. 'It has to happen. How it happens is down to you.'

'Ow... yes, alright, alright... I will... I will...' Absurdly, I tried to sound conversational, as though a negotiation had taken place, a decision reached by mutual compromise. 'Ow... just let go, let go.'

He let me go.

'Rightio. Come on then.' He sounded cheery as he headed back up the ladder.

Plunge Hill: A Case Study

A thought entered my head and I acted on it. I grabbed his ankle and hauled as hard as I could. He tried to hold on but his face connected with a rung and the shock caused him to fall face down on the ground, clutching at his nose and groaning, and slowly trying to rise, blood puddling darkly onto the concrete. I fell onto him awkwardly, pinning down his arms with my legs, my hands to his head. He had landed with his face at an awkward angle, half pressed into the mud embankment. I pushed down with all my strength. I had hoped he would drown in the mud but it was too dry. I heard him spit and retch as it ploughed into his mouth and worried the sound would bring the others. I snatched up something in my peripheral vision which I thought to be a rock but which turned out to be one of his boots, come loose in his fall, and struck him across the head with it. The fight went out of him, but it was only after I'd struck him a number of times and seen the flesh begin to give and felt the skull beneath it begin to yield that he went limp, and I slipped off him, exhausted. Then I rolled him into the trench in the floor, where my bed had been in the other foundations. I shoved the concrete mixer over him then upended it and watched as the contents – much blacker and thicker than I'd expected – poured over Clive, pooling over him, covering first his head and then his shoulders. I could not wait – I scrambled up the far side of the embankment, pulled myself through a gap in the hoardings and, unseen, made my way home.

There, I had a bath and put my clothes into a plastic bag and left. I never heard from Clive, and I returned a week later, in the night. There, where I'd left him, was the solid surface of Tarmac I'd had a hand in creating. Whatever his workmates did or didn't find out, I never learned – they never did anything about it.

It was, it now occurs to me, a year ago. It feels so much longer, a different lifetime. Perhaps it is a year ago today.

❧   ❧   ❧

Letter, handwritten. Unsigned, unaddressed, unsent. Dated 8th December 1971. Liversall collection.

Maurice – there's something about this time of year. The date. The second week in December. It feels important. They're all getting ready for the Winter Lights: I saw Blackheath putting up fairy lights in the windows of The Red Pony yesterday. There are little candles and decorations in the windows of all the houses in the village. Miss Liversall even sent me off to work today with a flask and a sandwich wrapped in a red napkin printed with stars. I know why this time is important to everyone else: it's their festival. But it is significant to me too, and I don't know why. Second week of December. What's so important about that? The desk next to mine, the one no-one uses, has been decorated with a row of winter flowers – cyclamens I think – around its edge. It looks like a shrine.

I'm sitting here at my desk scribbling away at this letter, very blatantly not doing any work at all and nobody seems to care because they're not doing any either – too busy putting lights up all over the place – as if to spite the power cuts.

I get up from my desk and wander the corridors whenever I feel like it. People glance at me and make way, as if they know who I am.

I am just daring Chapcott to call me to her desk and give me a roasting. I dare her! I dare her! She gave me a box of chocolates yesterday. Told me not to worry about anything, then turned away to cough into her handkerchief. I saw blood on it before she tucked it away. The corridor outside the palliative care ward has these huge plate glass windows that look out to the front of the hospital: you can see right down to the village, and across to the hills as they gather on the other side of the valley. And Kapoor is right. There are no sheep but always mutton to eat in the canteen. If I was in the palliative care ward – it smells like bleach and cigars and death – then I would jump right out of those windows. When I got back to my desk after my walk Chapcott was waiting and there were more presents. Chocolate. A half-used tube of cuticle cream. Candles piled up in the saucer. And a flower on my typewriter keys.

Kapoor has just been to see me. He was – I am almost certain of this, though even as I type it I can't quite believe it – drunk. He stank of porter and his hair was unkempt, his face unshaven.

'Well?' he said. He leaned over my desk. I leaned back, a little frightened of him. 'Did you read it? Do you know now. Do you know?'

'I know what she did to Clive,' I said. I'd read it the night before, sitting up in bed, an inch left on my candle. I'd guessed as much – almost seen it coming. Only a few pages left of her book to read now. Poor thing. 'It doesn't make her a bad person.'

Kapoor laughed. He pulled over an empty chair – its wheels squeaking against the floor – and sat down on it. The others ignored him. Nobody is deferential to him anymore.

'You are a genius, Bridget,' he said, 'or a saint. Or a combination of the two.'

'Don't make fun of me,' I said. 'It isn't my fault your experiments didn't work.'

'Right again, my dear. Right again. One can be a good person and still have blood on one's hands,' he pulled his hands out of his pockets – clean and neat, the nails filed short and even, the way doctors always do take care of their hands – and looked at them. 'And no, it isn't your fault that my experiments did not work.'

The flowers and trinkets and chocolate bars on my desk caught his eye.

'Ah. Yes. They had these little things for Holly too,' he said. 'They tell me it is part of the tradition. A way of showing respect. I wasn't here then. But I have something to give you myself.'

He fished around in the inside pocket of his jacket and produced a small bottle of pills.

'You can be a good person and still have blood on your hands. Tell yourself that, Bridget. Tell yourself that every day. These tablets are very strong. One or two of them taken with water in the morning will have a swift and pronounced effect on you.'

'The worm,' I said. 'The worm is coming, isn't it? Out of my dream.'

'I'm afraid so, yes.'

'Can't I leave? Escape. You could help me.'

'Oh, I wish I could,' he slapped a hand against his chest. 'I tried that before, you know, once. I need to think of the greater good, to weigh up the life of one person with that of a whole town of people.' He reached across, handing me the pills. I took the bottle from him.

'My mum had ones like these, after Maurice got ill and she got really worried all the time. They knock you out.'

'That's right, Bridget. My patients tell me that it isn't like you're completely asleep – you can still walk and talk. But you just don't seem to mind what is happening. It won't take away pain. It will just stop you minding about it.'

'Will they stop me dreaming?' I asked. I am sleeping so little now, sometimes I think the hospital itself and all of Plunge Hill is the bad dream, and the times at night, when the worm comes for me, are the reality.

'Your dreams will be over very soon,' Kapoor said, covered his face with his hand, and left. I think he was crying. I don't know what to make of him.

Plunge Hill: A Case Study

Anouk wasn't so bad. I can understand. Sometimes people do things – things that they don't mean to do, or plan to do, or even really want to do – because they think they've no other choice. It's a spur of the moment thing. Something gets into them and it just – happens. People shouldn't judge her for it. I don't.

I think I've got it. My head is so clogged – I don't believe I have been thinking properly for a long time now – but I think I know what it is now that's snagging me about the date. Winter Lights. Yes. And you Maurice. You. It was around this time of year that we went out skating, wasn't it? Even though you were very sick. Did you ask me to take you? We could both see all the other kids walking down the road towards it, holding their skates and their sleds and whatnot, and I think you must have been jealous. I put your feet into your boots and tied up your laces and buttoned up your heavy jacket for you. I did want you to be warm, didn't I?

Once you get to a certain point with leukaemia you are just buying time: everyone knows that. The doctors were torturing you and at the point where even turning over in bed made you black and blue with bruises. The whole house was covered in cards: as many saying *Get Well*

Soon as said *Merry Christmas* and both started to feel like an order that you didn't have a chance of obeying.

I carried you along the road to the park that day. I do remember that. Remember setting you down on wobbly feet at the edge of the frozen pond. Pointed out the skaters on the edge of the pond, and the kids who were sliding across the surface in their wellies and winter boots. I decided that it would probably be all right and if it wasn't all right that would probably be all right too. It only took a second and everyone rushed in to help but of course you were very very weak: your little heart wouldn't have stood the shock of the cold, that's what they said.

Miss Liversall has taken to her bed. I'm not allowed in her bedroom but I hear her in there, groaning and coughing. There's a bug going around, she said. Just a nasty cold. She said she'll be better after the Winter Lights.

It's nearly time to go home now. Mrs Chapcott says for me to get to sleep early and then come along very early tomorrow. First thing. She says she has a special dress for me to wear. So I feel part of things. Kapoor says I am a saint. A genius! Not a bad person. I am going to get to bed early, take some of the tablets tonight so I can get a proper night's sleep, and read the last part of Anouk's diary before I drift off. Hopefully the worm will stay away tonight.

Lots of love to you little Maurice x x x

Bridget

ᔰ   ᔰ   ᔰ

Anouk's diary, entry dated as previously. Liversall collection.

I must establish a clear record of what has just happened, and I must be precise. Brief yet precise.

I was called out. I was sitting alone in the office while the others were outside picking flowers in the grounds when I heard my name being called, a kind of sing-song calling. 'Anoo-ouk! An-ooo-ouk!' I ignored it at first, thinking it to be part of some prank against me. Or, no – rather I wanted to think that was why I was ignoring it. In truth I knew I was ignoring it because I didn't like to hear my name called out, to know I was being summoned.

J.M. McVulpin

I didn't like that they were all out there, in the gardens, engaging in whatever practice consumes them at Easter, with me in the office: ready, trapped.

And yet I could not very well ignore their calls. Their voices had moved from sing-song to earnest, jostling. 'Anouk? Anouk!' I stood up and made my way to the stairwell, the pane of glass in the door at the top of the stairs bright and blue with the midday sky.

'Come on, Anouk!'

'Don't be such a stick in the mud.'

'It's so lovely outside, Anouk!'

'Come on, Anouk!'

I trod slowly upwards, aspects passing into view through that window pane: the branches of a tree, the long train of a daisy chain, strewn across its branches, a garland of leaves and flowers atop a head, a flick parting, a serene face – it was, I saw, Chrissie, one of the quieter girls – and behind her, the others, each of the girls with their heads now decked with petals and leaves, each smiling, and beyond them others, people I'd seen around the town, men from the pub, people from other departments in the hospital, an elderly woman in a turban and a pink jumper. For a moment – as I opened the door and stepped out into the open, the breeze cool, the birdsong gentle, the smell of wild prettiness lulling – those placid serried faces seemed to me like the epitome of something I knew I had been searching for since coming to England but also before that, searching for for years: acceptance. Something tugged at my heart, compelling me towards them as though afloat.

This sensation left me when I sensed a presence flaring up close alongside me, someone lunging, and I felt a heavy blow to my ribs – so heavy it was almost intimate. I was flung onto my side and as I connected with the floor I could feel the wetness creeping across my clothes and I knew that the blow had been a knife. I looked up and saw that my assailant had been Blackheath. His hair was dishevelled by the attack yet still held a garland in place. In his hand was a scalpel.

'Oh… *Kristus… fitta…*' I gasped, my hand useless and tentative at the wound as it babbled. 'Help me… please, I've been hurt!' I looked at the typists from face to face, pleading with my clean hand, but each simply regarded me, watching as though the sight of me flailing, begging for help and bleeding was a kind of theatre and they the audience. 'Please!' I shouted, pivoting at them, my hand catching one the fronts of some of their dresses, leaving a red arc across the fabric.

That got a reaction. They stepped backward, gasping in outrage.

'My *dress!*'

'Oh my God!'

'She's *ruined* it!'

Mrs Chapcott emerged from within them, a log in her hands. Her eyes on mine, she lifted it up and brought it down across my face. I felt it split as it struck me and a blackness pounded up from behind my eyes.

I came to almost immediately, feeling myself being tugged at, the earth dragging beneath me as I was manoeuvred, a restriction around my chest as something was wound around me.

'What are you doing?' I said. I tried to move my arms but they were locked against my sides, my legs tethered together at the ankles. I tried to look up but I was in transit, being hoisted, I now knew, from a lying position to a suspended one: I was dragged into the air where I hung upside down. Directly beneath me was the well: I had been pullied aloft by a rope slung over the wooden frame which surrounded it. Beneath me I could see how immaculately decked out for Easter the grounds were. The flowers had been gathered together for displays. But, I saw, that was not quite the case. They had not been gathered, they were growing here – more flowers than had been here this morning, more than seemed even possible. Had they been planted? Is that what the other girls had been doing whilst I was downstairs typing away?

I spun slowly above the well. The faces that surrounded me were hard to decipher being upside down – the girls from the typing pool seemed interchangeable. The only one whose identity I was certain of was Mrs Chapcott who approached from the crowd and spoke to me with her face close to mine.

'I'm sorry, Anouk,' she said. She did not sound sorry. 'We're all sorry that it has to end for you like this.'

'Like what?' I said. 'What is happening?'

'Yes, we find it's best if they know a little bit about what's going to happen to them.'

'They?'

'Yes, well you're not the first, Anouk. We've done this many times. You might think you're special, that you're unique, independent, and so on, but… well, I'm afraid that's what they all think.'

'But you're—'

I was cut off by a low rumbling below me.

'What is that noise?'

'That noise you can hear is the worm.'

'The what?'

'Technically, it's not a worm. It has… limbs, of a kind, and what you could term a face. It's been here for as long as anyone can remember. Generations. You say goodbye to us today amid our Easter Parade and its accompanying customs, but I assure you there is a science to what you're about to go through. Not one I, nor anyone else, has been able to divine, but a simple science nonetheless: the worm makes people better.[21] It lives here, inside the hill, and its proximity makes those who live here well. It makes the badly sick go about their business as though they are in rude health, the old able to dance… Ah, I can see by your face that you have experienced this first hand. Perhaps a cut on your hand which healed too quickly, or a headache which vanished when you leant into the well…'

'It is what we used to call a miracle. But in order for it to be successful it requires something in return: blood, human blood. And, if the worm goes unfed for too long, well it emerges to seek it out. That rumbling you hear is its hunger. You have seen our little memorial for the disaster of 1827. That was when it last emerged, coming out of the well, or attempted to, killing nine locals in the process, three of them children, and destroyed a row of houses.

---

21   Freudians, take note.

Ever since, those who dwell here have agreed to feed it. And I work quite hard to find the right kind of blood.'

'The right kind?'

'The guilty kind. You killed Clive, we know that – we found it out. The last girl, Holly, she'd killed her mother. So I suppose you could say justice is being served. It was agreed they should be girls, as they tend to fight back less.'

'But that's... it's... well, it's monstrous.'

'We've tried everything we could. We've fed it sheep blood, horse blood, blood from dead bodies, we brought Dr Kapoor here to work on an alternative. But nothing has worked. And Anouk, you're just one person, one life given over to save many lives. Would you want children to die, homes to be destroyed? It's the way of the world – survival through unity. If Plunge Hill is to survive, we must give the worm what it wants.'

At that I simply couldn't help it. I laughed. Wheezing upside down laughing, feeling my face growing redder as I slowly twisted, taking in these upturned faces, their expressions serious and vaguely affronted by my giggling.

'Now, listen.' Mrs Chapcott's voice had hardened. She spoke matter-of-factly. 'I'm going to cut your throat. I'll slit it lengthwise and then across, like a cross. The plan is that you bleed out. It will be painful, at least at first. I'm never sure about the latter stages. Some of the girls seem almost serene by the time they reach the final stages.' She had produced the scalpel once again, and lifted it between us.

'Don't you touch me with that thing!' I spat at her and used what movement I had to twist away from her, the rope creaking quietly, and I furiously gyrated, effecting little more than a gentle swinging from side to side.

'Honestly, Anouk,' one of the girls in the crowds called out, 'it's best if you don't fight it.'

'I hate it when they thrash about like animals,' said another.

'Not exactly dignified, is it?' said another.

'The foreigners are the worst,' said another.

Chapcott steadied me with her free hand, lifted the scalpel with the other and pressed it into my neck. I shut my eyes tight and waited for it to begin – the slicing pain and the choking – so tight I could feel the blood rumbling through my temples, could *hear* it. But no pain or slicing or choking came. So I opened my eyes. All those present were stilled. The rumbling sound had moved outside my head and into the outside. An earthquake. It was getting louder.

'Do it now!' came a voice from the crowd behind Chapcott. She took hold of the ropes around me to pull me towards her, the knife raised to slash at me, when there was a sudden rushing of matter separating us. Something had burst from the well and was flowing up towards the sky at a great speed – something dark green and slime-like. At first I took it to be some sludge, volcanically expelled from the bottom of the well, but as I focussed I saw that it was not sludge. It had texture to it, form. I took it to be some stalk which had shot from the earth, some freak occurrence involving a beanstalk for which there would be an implausible but not impossible explanation. But then I saw that there were large translucent globs – suckers – along one side, and serrated outgrowths which looked to me like claws on the other.

The limb or tendril or whatever it was connected with the wooden frame over the well, splintering it and shuddering me downwards at an angle. As I was looking, one of the claws raced up at me and ploughed into my side, splitting the rope down my side and gashing my shin. I felt my leg spring abruptly free. Another claw passed through the rope suspending me and I was dumped downwards, my shoulder connecting with the side of the well. I rolled onto the grass.

Almost immediately someone was on me, one of the typists – Gloria – trying to wrestle me up.

'Come on!' she shouted over her shoulder. 'If we can just get her in—'

I pulled myself away from her and swept my foot across the backs of her legs which dropped her into a sitting position, Gloria's backside landing on the well. I saw a look of pleading as I put my hands against her shoulder and shoved her backwards into it. For a moment the rumbling fell silent and the tendril was motionless. But then the noise intensified. There was a blast of hot stinking blood from the well, flesh expelled into the sky like buckshot. A further tendril wormed out of the well, then a third. They thrashed at the ground and lapped at the side of the hospital, knocking dust off the brickwork and cracking windows.

Chaos gripped those gathered: some fell, some began to run away, others shouted, grabbing onto them, insisting they stay. I saw Mrs Chapcott seizing the typists, keeping them present, all their white robes now spattered with red. She pointed at me. I couldn't hear what she said but there was no need. I scrambled towards the hospital, pulling the door behind me shut. There was no lock and I held onto it as I felt them assemble and tug at the outside handle, the door flapping open away from me, a streak of spring daylight strobing alongside me, their faces and fingers visible. There was no way I could stop them and I began to make a plan in my mind for how I would prepare myself to die with dignity. But then a great impact on the door jolted me backwards, knocking it from my grip, almost sending me sprawling down the staircase. I jumped back up to push it shut again but saw immediately that the door was not open, although I could still hear them banging and shouting on the other side, and could see fingers trying to prise at a corner: a tendril had lashed against the door and buckled it in its frame, immovable.

'Round the other side!' I heard Mrs Chapcott say. People flickered past the windows, heading to the main entrance.

I turned and sprinted down the stairs, back into the typing pool. Already I could hear distant footsteps and voices down the corridor, growing closer. I paced the room, turning, looking. There was no other exit.

The footsteps echoing loud. A confusion of bodies spilling over one another to enter the room, their eyes wide, searching for me – several located me and they lurched in my direction. As they did so the lights above us flickered and then went out. I felt hands swarming over me as an arm clamped around my neck and hauled me sideways with such a force that I too blacked out.

I came to in Kapoor's office, the room lit by candles. He was sat at his desk, a silencing finger lifted to his lips. He nodded his head in the direction of the door. Then he stood up and knelt beside me.

'Our friends,' he whispered after a few moments. 'I believe they've moved on, but I cannot say for certain.'

'They wanted to kill me,' I said.

'Indeed,' he said. 'It is very important for them to do so. Gloria will do, I suppose, for a short time. The creature will be sated. But now you know...' He stood up and walked to a drinks cabinet in the corner of his office and poured a glass of some spirits which he set down beside me.

'Don't worry. It's not drugged,' he told me.

I took a sip.

'I can get you out of here, out of Plunge Hill,' he said. 'There is a route, a passage. It is narrow, but I think you will fit. But we need to wait until it is night before we can leave.'

And so this is where I have been sitting, writing this, my final missive. I shall hide you, diary – tuck you into this box of chocolates and stash you somewhere – where I hope whoever comes in my place shall find you.

꽃　꽃　꽃

Plunge Hill: A Case Study

Page torn from exercise book, in Bridget's handwriting, undated. Significant water damage. Liversall collection.[22]

I'm sorry I'm sorry

---

[22]   There were many items like this – scraps of paper, sometimes torn or screwed up into little crumpled balls, as if Bridget had intended to throw them away but couldn't quite bring herself to complete the action. All versions of the same thing: an apology, an admission of culpability, or at the very least, regret. What Bridget intended to indicate here, or indeed what we – or the authorities who took some interest in her brother's death – might infer from their presence amongst her papers remains open to debate.

One must be careful: the science of psychology must not speculate on what might have been, or what could be, only on what is. For precision, then: there were forty-eight items in the Liversall collection which contained nothing but the scribblings of an apology – and at least seventeen of them showed some evidence of minor or significant water damage. We might imagine Bridget scrawling these in the dark, or by candlelight. Perhaps even holding the papers underwater in the bathroom, during her somnambulant incidents. As we cannot ask Bridget, and even if we could, it is unlikely she would be willing – or indeed, able, to tell us – our speculation must appropriately end here.

By way of editorial note – as these scraps and fragments were so

similar to each other, and all undated, I kept them in a separate pile on my office floor, carefully smoothed out. One afternoon some weeks ago, as I was beginning the grim work of collating the case study you have just read, Dr Kapoor came into my office and found me kneeling before these papers, attempting to order them into some kind of sense. By this time, I believe, he had already made his decision to abandon his work at the hospital and search for a new position. He snatched up one of the pieces of paper and, on seeing what it contained, turned to me with fury written on his brow and, could this be correct – a man of science moved so? – tears starting in his eyes.

'You're not going to publish this?' he cried, tossing the piece of paper at me, where I still knelt before him on the floor. 'Are you insane? Or just cruel?'

'Parag, calm yourself. Calm yourself.' I heaved myself upwards, slowly, using the edge of the desk to assist me. My knees are not what they were. 'We've discussed this. It's for the good of the hospital.' I gestured around me – at the walls of my own shabby office, yes, but meaning to include the entire hospital itself – all its systems and methods, its staff and patients, and the glorious work we do here. Kapoor looked around him – at the draft plans for the ordering of the case study, the diagrams and flowcharts and the photographs of Bridget and her brother I had obtained by application to the local newspapers who had covered Maurice's death the previous year. He shook his head slowly.

'She was barely more than a child, Jack,' he said wearily. 'A confused child. The burden she carried. The sacrifice…'

I motioned towards my couch – indicated he should sit down, but he only drew a hand over his face and turned away, staggering down the corridor. That was the last time I saw him. It is out of affection and respect for him and his contribution to the work we do here at Plunge Hill, and in esteem of Bridget Shipley herself, that I give the last words of this volume to her. She was sorry.

Join the Society

The Eden Book Society is an ongoing book subscription brought to you by Dead Ink Books. Each book is written by a different author under a pseudonym and each year we select a different year from the society's history to reproduce. There's even a secret newsletter for subscribers only from our resident archivist digging through the Eden family records.

The 1972 books are written by: Andrew Michael Hurley; Alison Moore; Aliya Whiteley; Jenn Ashworth and Richard V. Hirst; Gary Budden; and Sam Mills.

If you would like to subscribe to The Eden Book Society please visit our website.

www.EdenBookSociety.com

The 1972 Subscribers

In 1972 the subscribers to the Eden Book Society were...

Adam Lowe
Adam Rains
Adam Sparshott
Adrienne Ou
Agnes Bookbinder
Aki Schilz
Alan Gregory
Alexandra Dimou
Alice Leuenberger
Alison Moore
Aliya Whiteley
Amanda Faye
Amanda Nixon
Andrew Pattenden
Andy Banks
Andy Haigh
Anna Vaught
Anne Cooper
Anthony Craig Senatore
Ashley Stokes
Audrey Meade
Austin Bowers

Barney Carroll
Becky Lea
Ben Gwalchmai
Ben Nichols
Ben Webster
Benjamin Achrén
Benjamin Myers
Blair Rose
blutac318
Brian Lavelle
C Geoffrey Taylor
C. D. Rose
Catherine Fearns
Catherine Spooner
Cato Vandrare
Chris Adolph and Erika Steiskal
Chris Kerr
Chris Naylor-Ballesteros
Chris Salt
Christopher Ian Smith
Clare Law

Colette
Conor Griffin
Damian Fuller
Dan Coxon
Daniel Ross
Dave Roberts
David Harris
David Hartley
David Hebblethwaite
Debbie Phillips
Dennis Troyer
Derek Devereaux Smith
Edward S Lavery
Elizabeth Nicole Dillon
Christjansen
Elizabeth Smith
Eloise Millar
Emily Oram
Eric Damon Walters
Erik Bergstrom
Erin C
Ex Somnia Press
Fat Roland
Françoise Harvey
Gareth E. Rees
Gemma Sharpe
Gia Mancini McCormick

Gina R. Collia
Green Hand Bookshop,
Portland, ME
Gregory Martin
Hannah allan
Harry Gallon
Hayley Hart
Heather Askwith
Helen de Búrca
Ian McMillan
Imogen Robertson
Inés G. Labarta
Jack Hook
James Smythe
Jamie Delano
Jamie Lin
Jayne White
Jean Rath
Jen Hinton
Jen Lammey
Jenna H.
Jennifer Bernstein
Jennifer Rainbow
Jim Ryan
Jo Bellamy
John P. Fedele
Jon and Rebecca Cook

Jon Peachey
Joseph Camilleri
Joshua Bartolome
Joshua Cooper
Justine Taylor
Karen Featherstone
Kate Armstrong
Kate Leech
Kathryn Williams
Kelly Hoolihan
Ken Newlands
Kiran Milwood Hargrave
Kirsty Mackay
Laura Carberry
Laura Elliott
Lee Rourke
Livia Llewellyn
Louise Thompson
Lucie McKnight Hardy
Madeleine Anne Pearce
Mairi McKay
Majda Gama
Margot Atwell
Maria Kaffa
Mark Gerrits
Mark John Williamson
Mark Richards

Mark Scholes
Martin van der Grinten
Matt Brandenburg
Matt Neil Hill
Matt Thomas
Matthew Adamson
Matthew Craig
Michael Cieslak
Michael Paley
Mitch Harding
Nancy Johnson
Naomi Booth
Naomi Frisby
Nathan Ballingrud
Nici West
Nick Garrard
Nick Wilson
Nicola Kumar
Nikki Brice
Nina Allan
Owen Clements
Paul Gorman
Paul Hancock
Paul Tremblay
Peter Farr
Peter Haynes
Philip Young

Ray Reigadas
Rhiannon Angharad Grist
Rhodri Viney
Richard Grainger
Richard Kemble
Richard Sheehan
Ricki Schwimmer
Rob Dex
Robb Rauen
Robert P. Goldman
Robin Hargreaves
Robyn Groth
Rodney O'Connor
Rudi Dornemann
Ruth Nassar
S. Kelly
Sanjay Cheriyan Mathew
Sarah R.
Sardonicus
Scarlett Letter
Scarlett Parker
Simon Petherick
Sophie Wright
Spence Fothergill
Stephanie Wasek
Steve Birt

Steven Jasiczek
STORGY Magazine
Taé Tran
Tania
Terra & Bill Jackson
The Contiguous Pashbo
The Paperchain Podcast
Thom Cuell
Thomas Houlton
Tim & Meg
Tim Major
Timothy J. Jarvis
Tom Clarke
Tom Jordan
Tom Ward
Tony Messenger
Tracey Connolly
Tracey Thompson
V Shadow
V. Ganjanakij
Verity Holloway
Vince Haig
Wheeler Pryor
Yvonne Singh
Zoe Mitchell

Also from the Eden Book Society...

Starve Acre
Jonathan Buckley

Richard and Juliette Willoughby live in an old farmhouse somewhere in North Yorkshire. The place has been called Starve Acre since anyone can remember and there is a local story about there being something buried in the field. A 'something' which prevents anything from growing there. Quite what it is varies from one person to the next a witch, or some tool once used by a witch, or the rope used to hang a witch but there is general agreement in the area that it is a place to be avoided. In fact, the locals blame Starve Acre for Juliettes illness, a degenerative mental condition that has transformed her into a vacant, ghost-like shell of her former self.

Holt House

L. G. Vey

It's a quiet house, sheltered, standing in a mass of tangled old trees called the Holtwood. Raymond watches it. He's been watching it, through a gap in the fence at the bottom of the garden, for weeks. Thinking about the elderly owners, Mr and Mrs Latch, who took him in one night when he was a frightened boy caught up in an emergency. Mr Latch showed him something that was kept in a wardrobe in the spare room. He can't remember what it was. He only knows how sick it made him feel. Raymond watches Holt House. He has to remember what he saw. He has to get inside.

The Castle
Chuck Valentine

Jon's dad was something of a pioneer in 1972, after writing a new kind of book – a book where readers could make their own choices and choose their own way through the story. Unfortunately, the idea was ahead of its time and his father died without ever finding the success he deserved.

It's the summer and, between signing on to the unemployment allowance, Jon's moved back to his hometown to help his mum cope with her grief. Contending with his own grief, he loses himself in his father's unpublished manuscripts. Fiction and reality blend perhaps a little too closely, and when he discovers a hidden appendix he finds that his father's imagination was more terrifying and more powerful than he could have imagined.

Judderman
D. A. Northwood

London, early-1970s: a city plagued with disappearances, football violence, Republican bombings, blackouts and virulent racism. A new urban myth is taking hold. Among the broken-down estates, crumbling squats and failed projects of a dying metropolis, whispered sightings of a malevolent figure nicknamed the Judderman are spreading. A manifestation of the sick metropolitan psyche, or something else?

Gary Eider's brother loved London, and was terrified by it. And now he's gone; he saw something no one else was willing to see. To find his brother, Gary must descend into the city and its violence, its hate, and its spite. There is something lurking there and it holds the answers to the city.